# Big Tom: Owlhoot

Mack Danvers was an orphan who, after an abused child-hood, was adopted by Tom Heineman, the notorious leader of the Loboes. Now Mack was schooled in the ways of the robber, rustler and gun-hawk and before long he could out-shoot almost anyone. He well and truly joined the owlhoot trail but despite all the crimes in which he became involved, there were still the vestiges of a decent human being.

He narrowly missed death on numerous occasions and was lucky to be rescued from the lynch mob. The turning point came when Tom, perhaps the worst of all sidewinders, told Mack to forgo his life of crime. It would be a long and bitter struggle, and death stalked him every step of the way. With luck, though, there would be someone waiting for him . . . .

# Big Tom: Owlhoot

JAY HILL POTTER

**A Black Horse Western**

ROBERT HALE · LONDON

© 1950, 2003 Vic J. Hanson
First hardcover edition 2003
Originally published in paperback as
*Gun Wolf* by V. Joseph Hanson

ISBN 0 7090 7277 5

Robert Hale Limited
Clerkenwell House
Clerkenwell Green
London EC1R 0HT

Typeset by
Derek Doyle & Associates, Liverpool.
Printed and bound in Great Britain by
Antony Rowe Limited, Wiltshire

# CHAPTER ONE

Mack Danvers was an orphan. He was only eighteen when he started running with the pack of owl-hooters who called themselves 'The Loboes'.

When Mack's uncle, the brutal Jed Benson, was bush-whacked and killed, doubtless by one of his many enemies, the law blamed the boy who hated him. But when, that still moonlight night, they came for the younker they discovered he had already upped and gone.

Two nights later in the middle of a howling storm a sodden wretched hungry kid stumbled into that camp in the Border hills and into the bear-like arms of Big Tom Heineman.

Big Tom was the leader of the Loboes, a six-foot-four, sixteen-stone giant with the strength of a grizzly and a gun-speed like the strike of a sidewinder. He took an instant liking to this frail, blond, hounded kid.

'The law!' he spat. 'You stay along with me, younker an' I'll make lawmen afraid of you before you're much older.'

For the first few months Mack's horizon was limited, bounded by the hills; looming before him constantly was the smooth rocky hump called the Ant Heap behind which the encampment was so effectively hidden. Beyond this was flat lush grassland, while for a mile or so behind the camp right across to the other side of the border stretched a desert of sand and scrub and cacti.

While the gang went out raiding, Mack stayed and helped Johnny Lee, the Chinese cook, and seventy year-old Panhandle Muggins and, up on the bluffs, the four guards who paced restlessly. Here at the camp Big Tom never took chances. The last posse that followed him never returned. But those tight-lipped bleak eyed guards could tell a tale about that if they chose.

Sometimes when the gang returned they were a man short and others were weak and blooded with wounds. One terrible night there were five men short and Big Tom was a savage, cursing monster with one arm in a ragged sling. Following this there was a period of inactivity when the men lounged about and smoked and gambled. They lived hair-trigger lives and were unused to inactivity. They quarrelled among themselves and drank rot-gut whiskey and bragged.

Mack heard gloating tales of savagery and pillage. To him they sounded glorious: years of ill-treatment at the hands of the late Jed Benson had inured him to brutality. When old Panhandle told him of the hated lawmen with whom he had tangled, Mack looked forward to the day when he too could get him a lawman's scalp.

Meanwhile Big Tom, whom he half-loved, half-feared, and wholly revered, was teaching him to draw and shoot. There could not have been a better teacher – or a more willing pupil. Like a kitten with cream the youth lapped up this poison: all the fanatical hatred of law and order and its exponents. Marshals, sheriffs, deputies, Rangers – 'hired killers' Big Tom called them. Kill them or they'd kill you he said. You had to be fast. The fastest-drawing man lived the longest. And you had to *keep* fast or maybe some-body would come along who figured they were faster – and prove it. Then there were the ranchers, the fat, happy, grabbing ranchers: Big Tom hated them almost as much. They and their milk-and-white daughters who went back East to get educated. And their hired thugs who crowded out the little man. Their lust for land and power. Nobody ought to be that rich – or live that long…. It was a garbled hymn of hate and the youth learned it, words and music. It tied up with the music of his first raid; the crackling and roaring of flames, the bawling of running cattle, the hoarse cries and the deep bass gun music. He was nearly nineteen then. He was immortal. He didn't get a scratch. And Big Tom was mighty proud of him.

Mack asked tentative questions of old Panhandle and received in answer a whispered tale. The old, old story of a man's love for a worthless woman and the sudden unpremeditated slaughter of her and her latest lover, of escape and the owlhoot trail where badmen in search of a leader flocked to the banner of this ruthless, fearless giant.

Big Tom had a cosy little set-up. The rustled cattle he ran over the border where, the brands blotted or changed, they were sold for ready money to buyers who asked no questions. But the Loboes did not stop at rustling. Stage stick-ups, bank robberies, some of them easy pickings, others which had to be worked out in detail days or weeks beforehand – they stopped at nothing. They were rich, richer than any mug of a cowhand, and they had their sprees, taking it in turns to go in twos or threes over the border or to some States town further West where there was no danger of them being picked up. Most of them had been 'Wanted' before they joined up with Big Tom. They were steel-nerved and trigger-happy.

The kid, Mack, wished to be just like them. For hours he practised drawing and shooting, his greased holsters tied to his thighs by whang-strings. He wore his serviceable twin walnut-handled Colts with their butts poking forward in front of his hips. He drew with a flick of his wrists. If a man mastered that particular draw properly it was the fastest and deadliest. Many other desperadoes used it, notably Wild Bill Hickock and Cherokee Jones. That draw was to make the kid, Mack, as notorious as they.

Mack figured in a couple of rustling-raids before he had his first spree. These particular raids were walkovers and the kid didn't get a scratch; as Big Tom put it jocularly, he hadn't been 'blooded' yet. He hadn't blooded anybody else yet either, which Big Tom reckoned wasn't so impor- tant, there was no need to kill any more dumb cowhands than was necessary. But the kid was getting touchy, he wanted a fling, so the big leader took him to San Antonio to work off that surplus energy. The results exceeded expectations, tho' Big Tom was mighty dubious about 'em. The results that is . . . .

As they rode away together on their little outing one member of the band scowled as he watched them. This was Johnny Logan. Johnny was thirty; big, lean, dark, coppery as an Indian. He was mean all the way through and clever to boot. He was Big Tom's chief *segunda*; to the giant only did he hold allegiance. It was he who usually rode out with Tom on the spree, altho', once at their desti- nation they were accustomed to split up, for Johnny was partial to the women and Tom was not. Anyway, this was the first time the big chief had ridden out of camp with somebody else. True, he had left Johnny in charge instead of the sour Pinto Cabot, but that did not compensate for the slight Johnny considered had been put upon him. And all because of that raw whippersnapper who had dropped out of the sky and, for all they knew, might be a Ranger spy. Stranger things had happened.

Big Tom dwarfed his companion. But Mack was spreading, his thinness was giving way to a wide-shouldered ranginess: the muscular co-ordination of the hard, cold gunfighter. The new boy was sharp too: Johnny Logan certainly had need to look to his laurels.

The man and the youth lounged about at the railhead, their hats over their eyes, unnoticed in the general melee until the San Antonio train came in. They saw to their horses at the stalls in the van (they didn't mean to leave them behind, considering they might need them). Then they went up front, chose a quiet corner and dossed down for a smoke and a chat.

A table across the other side of the car was taken by a couple of smartly-dressed gents who brought out cards and called across to the strangers to come and have a little flutter. Mack half rose. His companion nudged him and he settled again. 'No thanks, gents,' said Big Tom. 'I guess we're kinda tired.'

The smart men shrugged and let it go.

A little later Big Tom whispered 'They look like sharpers to me. We don't want any trouble. A moving train ain't an easy thing to get away from.

Mack grinned: 'I see your point, boss,' he said.

One of the men looked at him keenly. 'Maybe he thinks you're grinning at him,' said Tom. Mack pulled his hat over his eyes, closed them, and sank lower in the seat.

The two men carried on with their game. They certainly looked pretty slick. Presently they roped in a couple more players, oil-men by the look of their clothes. Big Tom was quick to note that first of all the oil-men won a couple of

hands apiece, then both of them began to lose steadily.
The Lobo leader shrugged his massive shoulders imperceptibly. None of his business. He liked taking other folks'
property and money himself. But he didn't like the
gamblers' way. Cold fish. But deadly when roused no
doubt. They had to be.

One of the  men looked across the car again. Maybe
you'll know me and my pardner next time you see us,
*hombre*, said Tom to himself.

The Southern Pacific 'Iron Horse' chugged into the
San Antonio terminus. Big Tom and Mack lighted down
and got their horses from the van. They lost sight of the
two gamblers and their disgruntled victims and thought
no more about them. They rode into town and got their
horses fed and stashed-up for the time being at a big 'dobe
livery-stable kept by a fat Mexican with big brass earrings
and no teeth.

Mack had never before seen anything quite like San
Antonio: the mixture of old Mexican, Indian and bawdy
Western civilization. He was intrigued by the ornate
Mexican temples with their shrouded beggars clustered
on their steps, behind them a cool, mysterious glimpse of
a dark interior. Gringos who entered these precincts were
frowned and scowled upon – and if they persisted, acci-
dents were liable to happen to them. The despised
'greaser' probably had freer rein in San Antonio than
anywhere else in Texas. His dirty 'dobe huts and clapboard
shacks were everywhere, he was a business man, a storekeeper or a beggar – never just a peon like many of his less
fortunate brethren in other parts of the Lone Star State.
There were plenty of Indians too, for the most part
dressed in the voluminous *serapes* whose use they had
borrowed from the Mex's. They did odd jobs or sold their

curios and interfered with no one. Every now and then an unprincipled Apache did a robbery or got himself a pale-face scalp but, for the most part, these were 'civilized' Injuns, the kind to make any of the old war-chiefs roll in their graves with utter disgust.

In San Antonio, which was rapidly growing in steady population, apart from the shifting mass of visitors, new buildings were going up all the time. Squat 'dobe Government offices, a new brick jail, and a host of eating-houses, saloons, honky-tonks and brothels of varying sizes. But Tom took Mack to one of the largest of these estab-lishments, one which combined all the dubious amenities of its smaller prototypes rolled into one and encased in a two-storey high 'dobe and wooden structure. It had about two dozen rooms and a towering, highly-painted false front which made the building look twice as high as it really was.

They sat down at a small round table in the huge assem-bly-room and ordered a hot meal and drinks from an obse-quious half-breed waiter. Mack took off his well-worn Stetson, ran his fingers thro' his long blond hair and, lean-ing back in his chair, looked around him. It was early yet so his keen scrutiny was not opposed by a lot of people. All along one side of the room ran a long, slightly concave bar with the inevitable brass footrail, its surface rubbed to a battered brightness by countless boots. At intervals there were brass spittoons too, half-full of sawdust. All along the back of the bar were large mirrors in gaudy gilded frames. If a guy at the bar kept his eyes straight in front of him nobody could sneak up on him from behind. At present there were three liquor-spillers in attendance; doubtless when things got really busy, there'd be three times that many. On the shelves to which the bartenders constantly turned was stacked every conceivable kind of tonsil-gargle, and right at the end of the bar, a corner where the hoboes could slink in unnoticed, a passable free lunch counter. One drink and you could eat as much as you liked of the onions, crackers, salt pork and corn bread.

In front of the bar was a wide cleared space for milling, and sometimes dancing, tho' the dance-hall proper was just down the street. In the corner opposite the free-lunch was a raised dais with a piano and room for other musicians. There were plenty of tables and chairs for dining and drinking purposes and almost as many gambling layouts of all kinds sprinkled around. People could play poker or suchlike on any table they fancied  but if they wanted something more specialized there were layouts for faro, *monte,* roulette, keno, checkers, 'Chuck-a-luck', dice, and occasional lotteries.

Mack suddenly nudged Big Tom, 'Look who's over there,' he said. His companion looked in the direction of the discreet inclination of the younker's head and spotted in a far corner the two gamblers of the train. By the look of things they were operating a faro layout.

The arrival of the eats. As they tucked in Big Tom said:

'I figured them ginks were sharpers. I've never seen a faro set-up that wasn't crooked. But there's something about it that gets you. I used to be quite a boy for "buckin' the tiger" myself.'

'I'd kind of like to have a spin myself,' said Mack.

'So you shall, boy,' said Tom suddenly, jocularly. 'So you shall.'

Mack left it at that and attacked his substantial helping of liver, potatoes, 'sinkers' and peas. The latter were the Chicago canned variety, hard as buckshot – he spat a few of them disgustedly in the direction of the nearest spittoon. The only way to get them down was to take them like pills, with a swig of coffee. The rest of the meal was good, however, and the partners wound it up with a plate of steaming *frijoles* and a jug of syrup.

Afterwards they both lay back in their chairs with signs of contentment. Big Tom produced a sack of 'makings' and rolled himself a quirly. He passed the sack across to Mack. They lit up. They chatted desultorily, their bellies full. But pretty soon the volatile Mack was raring to go again.

'How about that crack at buckin' the tiger,' he said.

'You go on along, son,' said Big Tom benignly.

Mack grinned and rose. As he crossed to the layout manipulated by the two train-gamblers he knew the big feller would not be far behind him.

If the two gamblers recognized him neither of them gave any signs of doing so. The elder, who with his pencilled moustache and long black sideboards certainly looked the part, was shuffling. He placed the pack face uppermost in the faro box, which, a conventional type, was open at the top. The top card of the deck was the king of diamonds. The box was slightly larger than the cards and the end nearest the gambler was open so that with a long white forefinger he could slide the pasteboards out smoothly to deal. It was the usual set-up, it looked straight enough, but Mack remembered what his big pardner had said. He got closer to the table to watch the first play, figured to join in himself a mite later.

The dealer's pard stood beside him keeping a watchful eye on the dealing and the players and generally helping-out by paying and collecting. Trouble was it was quite a job for a player to watch both gamblers as well as his own cards. The sidekick was a younger fellow, pale-faced, handsome and thin as a whip.

'Place your bets, gentlemen,' he said in a curiously soft, cultured voice, then called the phase that all inveterate gambles love to hear, 'The sky's the limit'. The bank seemed to be 'in the chips' …. But when they were that open-handed in faro it was Mabel's combinations to a pinch of snuff that the layout was 'rigged'.

After the first round the bank broke about even. Looking up from the game Mack perceived that Big Tom had moved to a position just back of the gamblers. Evidently neither of them had spotted him. They were cold deadly players, not the type to let their attention wander from the game. Big Tom sat down at an empty table. From there he could watch their every move. He crouched down unobtrusively in the chair, concealing his bulk. Mack noted that his arm hung over the chair-back, the lax fingers dangling near to his gun-belt. It was a favourite sitting position of his. You had to get up mighty early to take Tom by surprise – even when he looked as dopey as a hibernating grizzly.

Mack figured he'd have himself a whirl. He got his belly up against the table and placed his bet. He lost. The next time he won. Looking up as he raked in his chips he caught the young gambler looking at him keenly. He grinned. There was no answering smile. These bozoes took their work seriously. Mack did not look towards Tom. He knew the big man was watching every move. Maybe this was that thing so rare in the West: a straight faro layout. Played that way the odds were with the customer: small wonder that most operators had their tackle rigged.

Mack placed his bet again. This time he lost. Again the young gambler looked at him keenly as he raked in the

14

chips. It was a cool supercilious look as if to say 'I'll know you again if I see you fellow, but I'm not really interested.'

This time Mack did not grin at him. He felt more like smashing his face in. To relieve his feelings he plunged again, heavily with almost all he'd got. Being only a fledgling where these grown-up parlour games were concerned he didn't realise that he was doing just what the other younker wanted. It was an old con-man's trick: antagonizing the customer until he plunged defiantly – up to his neck.

The older man began to draw from the box, watched avidly by Mack, who had by far the bigger stake on, and the other players. Something impelled Mack to look up and with a little inward start he dropped his eyes again. Big Tom was on his feet and standing, unnoticed by the two men, close behind the layout.

Mack watched the gambler's long white fingers smoothly, swiftly manipulating the pasteboards. But his mind wasn't on the game now and his eyes flickered. He braced himself. Big Tom wasn't standing there for fun.

Suddenly the big man made his play. His cold level voice cut thru' the general babble. 'Brother, pick up that horsehair.'

It was Greek to Mack, but the two gamblers reacted to it quite unpleasantly. The older one turned, his hand streaking downwards. Then he looked into the snout of Tom's Colt. The younger man did not seem to move but a small derringer, which had been cunningly hidden up his sleeve, suddenly appeared in his hand.

Mack took a step backwards from the table and drew. His gun boomed as it  scraped leather. The gambler screamed and his gun spun from his hand. He caught hold of his smashed wrist with his other hand. The blood

15

gushed thru' his fingers. He stood swaying for a moment, his eyes dilated, his face yellow, then he slumped forward across the table in a dead faint.

'Good for you, younker,' said Tom.

He reached forward and slashed out with his gun. The sharp barrel laid the other gambler's temple wide open. He tumbled from his chair and fell to the boards on his face. He lay still.

Big Tom picked something up from the mouth of the dealing-box. He held it up. It was almost invisible in his big hand.

'Horsehair,' he said. 'It's a new trick to tie half-a-dozen o' the best cards together so they don't part during the shuffle. Then he cuts the tie on this sharp plate at the bottom o' the box. You were bein' fleeced, gentlemen. Get your money back.'

Smoking gun still in his hand Mack made sure of his pile. He backed away from the table. Tom joined him. They didn't like being crowded.

The big man said: 'Me an' my pard've got some urgent business. I wouldn't advise anyone to follow us.'

Nobody argued with them as they backed thru' the doors.

'Come on,' said Tom. 'Before the law gets around. We want no truck with them.'

'Yuh durn tootin',' said Mack.

The fat Mexican at the livery stable was surprised to see them back so soon.

'Saddle up, *hombre*, pronto,' said Tom and showed him a greenback which made his little black eyes pop.

He obeyed with alacrity and pocketed the money. His face was a toothless gap. But he hadn't been quick enough, for as the two men led their mounts from the

16

stables they were accosted by two more *hombres*.

'Look like Rangers,' whispered Tom as they saw the two men approaching. 'Leave the talkin' to me. If they're awkward get up close and slug 'em. Don't shoot unless you have to – we don't want the whole boiling of 'em down on our ears.'

Then he had to cut his little speech off short. The foremost Ranger was lean and lanky. He said: 'You're jest the gennulmen we wanna see.'

'Yeh, pardner, what can we do for you?' said Big Tom affably.

The beanpole flipped back his shabby vest and showed his badge.

'You did a bit o' shooting back there didn't you? Them two gamblers is kinda mussed-up.'

'They asked for all they got – an' more, said Tom mildly. 'They were cheatin'. Using the tie-up trick.'

'We know that,' said the beanpole, just as mildly. 'We ain't blamin' yuh none, suh. But we'd like to hear more about it.'

His stockier pard suddenly chimed in rather brusquely. 'What Bob wants, suh, is for you to come down to the post with us an' sort of report.'

'But, boys, there's no need for all that. Them gamblers drew first. It was self-defence. We got witnesses to say so. An' the men ain't dead are they?'

'Nope. But whether it was self-defence or not we still wanna report.'

'I've given you one, haven't I?' said Big Tom. 'You see, boy, we're kind of in a hurry. We ....'

'Won't take but a few minutes to get to the post, suh,' said Bob. 'I guess you'd better come on along.' He smiled, standing squarely in the big man's path, his

17

thumbs hooked in his belt.

His smile did not fade as he looked down at the Colt which had magically appeared in Tom's hand. It was pointed directly at his lean middle. 'Step on one side, pardner,' said Tom. He wasn't smiling.

Mack watched Bob's pard. He looked surprised but he didn't make a move.

'I ain't movin', big boy,' said Bob. 'That kind of play ain't gonna get you nowhere.'

Tom whipped up and across with the gun, treating the Ranger as he had treated the gambler. Bob's face gushed blood as without a sound, he went down. His pard moved and Mack kicked him hard across the shins. He yelped and staggered forward. Mack drew and hit him across the head, crumpling his sombrero. He joined his lean companion in the dust.

The fat Mexican stableman yelled 'Murder', and tried to get past Mack. The young Lobo slashed at him; the gunbarrel hit him behind the ear and, with a groan, he fell heavily on his face.

Both men mounted. 'Come on,' said Tom. He lashed his horse furiously with a quirt. They set off at a gallop, sending the dust of San Antonio up in clouds behind them.

'We gotta keep movin' fast,' yelled Tom. 'Them Rangers is poison once they get on your trail.'

Mack remembered the lean Bob's face as he went down from Big Tom's blow. He guessed there was one Ranger who wouldn't forget in a hurry. The big Lobo had marked him for life.

'We're a long way from home, Mack,' said Tom. 'But we've got to ride. We can't risk jumping a train. Leastways not until we get outa this territory.'

It was almost dawn when they did catch a train at a little tank town stop on the branch line. They hadn't slept all night so took it in turns to drowse by daylight.

They hopped off again before they reached their destination. As they jogged along on the last lap of their journey Mack asked Tom again about the faro tie-ups trick.

'It's purty new,' said the big man. 'The man who keeps the big Casino in Austin showed it to me when it first came out about twelve months ago.'

Mack wondered what the Lobo leader was doing in the Austin Casino at that time but he knew it was no use asking.

The speaker continued: 'They've got some of the smartest operators in the States in that Casino. The tie-up ain't easy, it needs a lot of practise an' a man's gotta be fast. How it's done is this way … About half-a-dozen or so of the best cards are put together and pierced by a very thin needle. Then the short piece of horsehair is threaded thru' and tied. If it's done carefully nobody 'ud notice, particularly the way those people whisk the cards around. No matter how much they're shuffled, you see, them cards stick together – until the dealer puts 'em in the box. Most o' them boxes are, as you know, made of brass, the one back there was. Wal, the edge o' the bottom plate is sharpened specially so that the dealer can snap the horsehair on it and free his cards. Naturally he deals them to himself – half-a-dozen or more of the best cards in the pack. He can't miss.'

'Sounds like a good set-up,' grinned Mack. 'You'll have to teach me. Maybe I'll take it up as a profession.'

'I guess I ain't much good at it myself,' confessed Tom. 'Neither would you be. You ain't got the temperament.'

The Lobo leader sighed and lay back in his seat. 'Wal,

anyway, son, you bucked the tiger mighty fine. An' you also got yourself "blooded" in an admirable way. Thet young gambler was fast but he never had a chance.'

'I ain't blooded,' said Mack. 'I didn't get a scratch.' Tom wagged his shaggy head slowly and pityingly.

'That ain't what I meant. Gettin' blooded is just like when a tenderfoot hunter makes his first kill. It's a sort of initiation – see what I mean.'

Mack nodded. 'Yeh ... Yeh.' He often wondered where Tom had got his high-falutin' talk from. At times he didn't seem the same man. Who was he? Where did he come from? Even old Panhandle, who knew some of the facts of his story, did not know that. Still, Tom was interesting to talk to when he was like this. His speech became subtly different and he didn't sound like a common cowhand, which was what most of the Loboes had been before they hit the owlhoot trail.

Mack figured he'd ask him some more about this initiation business. He opened his mouth – then shut it again without saying anything. Big Tom was fast asleep.

Mack eased his gun in its sheath before he leaned back a little. He looked around him. Then while his leader slept he kept his eyes wide open by a conscious effort. His was the eternal vigilance of the owlhooter ... The gun-wolf. It was the life he had chosen. It seemed now that he had never known another.

# CHAPTER TWO

The gang were surprised to see them back so soon.

Johnny Logan said: 'What's the matter, boss, does our boy Mack set too hot a pace for you?'

The words were innocuous but the tone in which they were spoken was sneering.

Mack said: 'Maybe you'd ....'

Big Tom's voice cut in. It was jocular but both the younger men knew they were being talked down. 'Nope. But it was too hot for two other gents I could mention.'

He recounted the tale to the huge delight of the rest of the band who crowded around Mack slapping him on the back and using such terms as 'ring-tailed bobcat', 'salty young coyote', 'hornery young skunk' ....

The disgruntled Logan lent his voice to the rest but he kept away from Mack. He didn't touch him. Maybe he would sooner slap the younker's back with a cleaver in his hands.

Mack had sensed the other's antagonism for sometime. He wasn't a weak raw kid now and he wouldn't stand ramrodding. Logan hadn't made a move yet but Mack reckoned he would sooner or later. He'd be ready for him.

'I guess we need some shut-eye,' said Tom. 'Take it easy, boys. We'll be gettin' ready to ride again in another couple o' days or so.'

That was good news. But nobody asked questions. They knew their leader would tell them in his own good time.

Next morning after breakfast Mack went to the back of the cookhouse to get in a bit of his usual daily lead-slinging practise. Often some of the boys came with him and there was desultory competition. Right now there was a crap-game running in the bunkhouse. Mack figured he'd had enough of gambling for a bit so he left them to it. His only onlooker was Johnny Lee, the Chinese cook, who was rapt in admiration of such wizardry. To Johnny guns were tools of the devils but he was crackshot with a frypan or a skillet as many of the boys could ruefully testify. But he was a wonderful cook and except for occasional furores they left him in peace.

Johnny tossed cans and bottles of every shape and size on the dump behind his shack so Mack was never short of targets.

This morning he began by practising his marksmanship with the new test he had recently set himself. He took half-a-dozen small cans and strolling with them until Johnny thought he was walking plumb out of camp he placed them in a line along a grassy mound. Then he came back.

The tins now, at that distance, were just tiny squares winking in the early-morning sunshine. They were a mite out of revolver range, which was just how Mack wanted them. He had figured out the fraction of an inch elevation of his gun-muzzle that would take care of that. He drew both guns.

He brought them forward, his elbows slightly bent, and thumbed the hammers. The double-blatter of shots made Johnny Lee wince and clutch with trepidation at the jamb of his doorway as if he thought the shack would collapse around his ears. Six shots close together and the little squares winked and vanished. All except one. Mack cursed and thumbed again three times. The tin did a frenzied parabola and disintegrated.

Mack lifted his smoking guns and blew the powder-dust from their muzzles. Then he began his jaunt once more, taking with him another can to replace that last one he had just shot to pieces.

As he was returning to his position Johnny Logan came around the corner of the cookhouse.

'Howdy, Johnny,' said Mack.

'Howdy, Mack,' said the lean dark man, more affable than usual. 'That you doin' all the shootin'?'

'Yeh. Jest practisin'.' Mack turned to face the cans once more, drawing his guns.

Before he could fire a blatter of shots made him start. The tins disappeared like a line of gophers going back into their holes. Mack turned again, his ears singing. Johnny Logan grinned at him, his white teeth flashing wolfishly in his Indian-like face. He had a smoking long-barrelled Colt in each hand.

'Nice shootin',' Johnny,' said Mack. 'Your turn to stack 'em up again.'

Logan pulled a wry face. 'Walk all over there? Not me.' He holstered his guns and crossed swiftly to the rubbish dump. He picked up a can and, turning, tossed it high in the air.

This time Mack's guns spoke first. By the merest fraction of time he had beaten the other man to the draw. The can did a cartwheel in mid-air, then seemed to pause in space as the slugs drummed into it. As it began to fall both men were blasting away at it. It was a very sorry-looking can when it finally reached the sod once more.

The two men were so engrossed in their game that they did not see old Panhandle Muggins and Big Tom's sour right-hand man, Pinto Cabot, join Chinese Johnny Lee at the back door of the cookhouse. Both young men reloaded their Colts.

Then Logan took a coin from his pocket and spun it in the air. Mack slapped leather, firing from his hips. What was left of the coin fell in three tiny glittering pieces.

Then it was Mack's turn to spin. Logan's shooting was quite up to the mark. His silver bits and pieces joined the others in the dry dust.

Then he held up his finger. 'One,' he said.

Mack nodded and tossed another dollar. Logan drew and fired once. The coin gyrated, glittering in the sunshine, then dropped like a stone. Logan picked it up. It was drilled clean.

He tossed it again. Mack's draw was brilliant. Again the misused dollar faltered and flashed. When they scrutinized it the hole in its centre was a little bigger. Mack grinned and threw it high. They both drew, firing, it seemed, wildly – but with deadly precision.

Over at the cookhouse old Panhandle said: 'There goes two o' the saltiest, shootingest young coyotes in the state o' Texas.'

'Yeh,' said Pinto with unconscious irony, 'I hate to think what'll happen if they start shootin' at each other.'

It did indeed seem as if they were testing each other's lead-slinging capacity. The gun-music went on for quite a while. As shooting-up Uncle Sam's legal tender proved fair to be an expensive game they went back to the rubbish-heap to find targets. Finally Big Tom came barging round the back and told them to cut out the ruckus, for Pete's sake – and other unprintable reasons.

'We wuz runnin' out o' cans, anyway,' said Mack.

The game over, Johnny Logan strode away without

another word. He didn't like being told to stop, even by the boss. Mack looked after him quizzically.

Big Tom turned on Johnny Lee who was still hovering at the cookhouse door. 'What you doin' there, yuh grinnin' heathen. Get back to your chores.'

Johnny went in mortal fear of the big booming boss. He rolled his almond eyes and scuttled out of sight. The immediate clatter of pots and pans signified his haste to soothe the boss's wrath.

Big Tom looked again at Mack. 'Shootin' off slugs all over the place,' he said scornfully. 'Did yuh think it was the Fourth of July?'

'I gotta keep in practise ain't I,' said Mack innocently.

'You don't need no practise in throwin' lead,' Tom told him. 'Wastin' ammunition. All you've got to do is keep your guns well-oiled. Your holsters too. An' practise your draw – keep on practising your draw.'

'Yeh, boss,' Mack grinned again. He was like a lean, cocky young bantam cock. Mighty sure of himself. He hadn't figured out altogether yet what nasty pitfalls might be in front of him.

Garret's Gulch was an up-an'-comin' little cowtown. A branch line of the Pacific Railway ran thru' it and every month or so a freight-train stopped there to pack on cattle from the small ranches which abounded thereabouts. With the cattle came the cowboys, and when the job was done, and the train cheered on its way, for one night at least 'The Gulch' was a 'wide-open town'.

There was shootin' an' fightin' but nobody ever got seriously hurt for the Gulch was a peaceable little community and the rough and ready cowhands, like big kids most of 'em, respected this fact. Many of them, if they had any cash left after the night's jollifications, trundled down to the bank to put it in the safe fatherly hands of the manager, Jeb McCloud. Then with much shrieking and whooping and firing of guns in the air they left the town and it seldom saw them again till the next trail-drive.

Garret's Gulch was proud of its bank. It was proud too of its Jeb McCloud; bank-manager, president, and also unofficial mayor and justice. A plump, white-haired aristocratic-looking man was old Jeb. A little complacent maybe, a little pompous, but a good man, a trustworthy man. They'd back him to the hilt, fight for him if need be, and in the West in these lawless days, people seldom forgot how to fight.

Little wonder the kindly, autocratic Jeb became more aristocratic, more complacent with every passing day, never dreaming of the leading role Fate had allotted to him in a little drama, all worked out by a man much cleverer than Jeb many weeks before it was enacted ....

It all began, tho' nobody knew it at the time, when the first cowboys began to troop into the street and greet the sunny morning with bleary eyes, to kiss their girls for the last time, to saddle up their horses regretfully, to meander down to the bank to see old Jeb before they went.

Opposite the bank was Caleb Slattery's emporium where, it was boasted, you could buy anything from a repeating rifle to a ribbon for your gel's hair. Most of the cowhands visited Caleb too to buy any of the little things they wanted to take back to the ranch with them. All that morning the visits to Caleb and Jeb went on, the exodus, the yellin' and the shootin'. Gradually the town became quieter and the townsfolk, heavier in pockets but frayed of nerves, heaved sighs of relief.

The last bunch of waddies who reined their horses outside the bank comprised about seven in all. The one who seemed to be the acknowledged leader was red-haired and very big, a flaming giant among men.

They did not call on Caleb and the old storekeeper watched them curiously thru' his window. He couldn't recollect having seen any of these boys before …. Still, lots of the ranchers had new boys. Saddle-tramps most of 'em. Maybe they'd bring their custom over a mite later when they'd seen Jeb McCloud. They pushed and joshed each other outside the bank. They seemed in no hurry. The big man was grinning and gesticulating. Old Jeb dismissed them as a pack of jackasses and turned back to his shelves. But if he had heard what the big feller was softly saying amid his grins and gesticulations, the old man would not have been so complacent. That was the trouble with Garret's Gulch. Being so far from the border and the badlands they thought themselves immune from any depredation ….

Big Tom Heineman had dismounted from his horse and had one foot on the board steps. He said:

'Now you all know what to do. Johnny, you stay by the door …. You three lounge about an' keep your eyes peeled. Mack an' Pinto, you come with me.'

Four of them crossed the sidewalk quickly. At the door Johnny Logan stopped and turned half-round. He leaned against the door-post, his thumbs hooked in his belt, his head bent, his hat low over his eyes. Two other men hung around the horses, chatting and smoking; their companions left them and sat down on the edge of the sidewalk.

Big Tom led Pinto Cabot and Mack onwards and swung open the door of the bank. The three men strode into the cool, dusky interior.

Jeb McCloud always received his visitors in person. Now he came bustling forward, his smooth plump face beaming, his white hair shining like a nimbus around his head.

27

Then he paused for a moment. More new boys. Altho' that big one did look kind of familiar. Then he came closer.

'Come right in, boys. Glad to see you. I ....' Then his voice broke, stopped, started at higher pitch, excited: – 'Why, Tom, I didn't know you ....'

'That's enough,' barked Big Tom. 'Keep your mouth shut.' A gun appeared in his hand. His face had drained suddenly of its coppery colour but his eyes were burning. 'I didn't know it was you, Jeb – but that's not goin' to stop me.'

Mack and Pinto spread out each side of him, menacing the rest of the staff with their drawn guns.

'Give me the keys to the deposit-box, Jeb,' said Big Tom hoarsely.

The banker's ruddy face had paled too. His eyes were wide and pained. Silently he produced the keys and handed them over.

'Where is it?'

Jeb jerked his head in the direction of his office.

'Watch him, Pinto,' said Big Tom. 'Mack – get over to the counter.'

Pinto turned one gun on the banker. The other hung loosely ready to swing into action. Mack went over to the counter, where three clerks watched him warily. On the little shelves behind them were piles of notes and coins they had been engaged in counting.

Mack took a leather bag from his belt and tossed it to the nearest clerk.

'Put it all in,' he said. With one hand he lifted the trap and went round behind the counter. From under there he fetched more bills, also a gun which he tucked into his belt.

The clerk with the bag, a frail young fellow, was doing his job with nervous haste. Mack looked the other two over.

'Raise your hands,' he said.

Two pairs went up, one pair very reluctantly. The owner was a well-built specimen, but he didn't seem to be armed.

Mack looked him straight in the eyes. 'Don't try anythin', pardner,' he told him. 'We don't like tuh shoot unless we have to.'

'I'll remember you,' said the other, eyes blazing.

Mack felt like dropping his guns and giving him a run for his money with his fists. 'Quiet,' he said.

The frail young man had filled the bag. Mack took it from him and went back to the customers' side of the counter.

Big Tom was coming from the office. He swung a bulging bag in his left hand, his gun in the other.

He said: 'You boys behind the counter 'ud better come out front.'

The three men filed round. 'Lie down on your faces. You too, Jeb.'

The four men did as they were told, the old banker, his face still white, grunting a little. He seemed suddenly older and broken-up.

'I should advise you to stay down there for  bit,' said the Lobo leader. 'If either of you show a hair my boys'll start shootin'.' He jerked his head to Pinto and Mack. 'Come on!'

They backed out together, Tom and Mack passing thru' the doors a little in advance of Pinto. Even so Mack saw one of the clerks roll over, tugging a derringer from his breast. Then Pinto was in the way. Both he and the clerk fired together. The clerk, it was the pugnacious one who threatened Mack, gave a choking cry and subsided again. Pinto's leg went from under him, he went down on one knee.

Jeb McCloud was rising yelling: 'Help! Help!'

Pinto fanned the hammer of his gun savagely. The old banker rose convulsively to his full height, stiffened there, his blue eyes wide and accusing beneath the halo of white hair. Then he fell.

Big Tom stood like a man petrified until the limping Pinto barged into him.

'Boss!' said Mack.

Tom turned mechanically. The three men ran across the sidewalk, Pinto, dragging his wounded leg, in the rear.

Johnny Logan joined them. The other three were already mounted, their hard, practised eyes raking the street. Not until Tom, Mack and Johnny had mounted did they realise that Pinto was not with them.

He had fallen on the steps.

'Come on,' snarled Tom, wheeling his horse.

One of the men fired as the barrel of a gun poked from the doorway of Caleb Slattery's stores.

'Pinto!' said Mack.

Old Caleb opened up from inside his shop. A slug whisked Johnny Logan's hat off.

'Come on,' barked Tom, setting spurs to his horse.

'Tom!'

'Tom,' screamed Pinto.

Mack turned. Pinto was trying to get up, one hand holding on to a step, the other held out beseechingly for help. His face was contorted with agony and awful frustration.

Mack was half-out of the saddle when Big Tom's horse barged into him. Mack saw Tom's sneering contorted face as the gun in the big man's hand spoke twice. Pinto's eyes opened wide with terrible surprise, his face crumpled, he uttered two sharp sobs like a stricken animal, then the face disappeared as he fell forward and somersaulted down the steps.

Big Tom bawled in Mack's ear. Then he was gone. Down the street with the others in a cloud of dust. A bullet plucked at Mack's sleeve. He came out of his stupor. He saw the old storekeeper's head disappear again as the boys retaliated. Other people were coming down the street, but on foot. Mack's horse was bounding forward as turning, he sent a stream of lead screaming over their heads, scattering them to cover.

Another figure appeared at the door of the bank then dodged back as Mack fired. He had another glimpse of the remains of Pinto, like a bundle of rags at the bottom of the steps, then he was away from it all, striving to catch up with the others. He did so. They met no more opposition. Too late the townsfolk of Garret's Gulch had realised that these boys were not just another bunch of cowhands firing guns into the air ....

The bunch rode hard. They were a long way from home. They were silent, each with his own thoughts, not jubilant as they usually were after a successful coup. Young Mack Danvers' mind was in a turmoil and thru' all the mixed up jumble flashed pictures that would not leave him. He saw them over and over again, the accusing, pathetic face of a white-haired old man dying on his feet; the terrible, so similar look on another face – a body tumbling down the steps like some soggy sack of meal. These things would not leave him and they awoke strange feelings in him which he could not explain. Words echoed in his brain too, the only words spoken by Big Tom since they left the bank, puzzling words to come from the mouth of a man who had just wantonly slaughtered his right-hand man, words spoken harshly, forced thru' clenched teeth:

'I must be gettin' soft.'

They reached the hideout late that night, tired, silent, desperate men. They hadn't had the whiff of a posse. Everything had gone off without mishap – except, of course, for Pinto. It had all been so easy – like taking candy from little kids. They were rather deflated desperate men. During the journey attempts at conversation had been made by all – except Big Tom and Mack Danvers – but had pretty soon died out.

The loot was prodigious and the camp was overjoyed. Until somebody asked about ol' Pinto. By that time Big Tom had gone to his cabin. The tale was told, without embellishment or comment, by Johnny Logan. Emotions were mixed. Nobody had ever been able to really figure the boss. Still what's the odds? The money was here wasn't it? Piles of it. Pinto had been a sourpuss, anyway .... We all die sometime.

Mack Danvers took no part in any of the conversation, sitting with his back against a tree moodily sipping hot coffee. Neither did Panhandle Muggins, who was a sorely troubled old man. Johnny Logan and the other three men who had been on the raid got drunk with the rest. But Mack remained sober, viciously so, refusing with curses any drink that was offered him. He was evidently in a fighting, killing mood. After a bit they wisely let him be.

Finally he rose and slouched away. He went to the cookhouse, to his old friend Johnny Lee. He was sick of the singing coyotes round the fire. With the heathen Chinese cook, who spoke little and smiled a lot with philosophic calm and age-old wisdom, he found a modicum of peace. But he did not sleep well that night. Those pictures were still with him. And with them now, looming thru' them more and more was an unfamiliar, and yet terribly familiar face, a broad sneering face that was like a twisted parody of the features of Big Tom Heineman.

The following morning, rising was late at the hideout. When Johnny Lee made a hideous din with a frypan and wooden spoon nearly everybody was still bunked down.

For all the notice they took they might have been Egyptian mummies. Panhandle took the implements of noise from Johnny and marched into the bunkhouse banging them together and yelling hoarsely: 'Come an' git it, you stinkin' coyotes. Come an' git it.'

Then he turned and ran, but not before one wildly thrown boot had hit him on the back of his head. But they were roused, and grumbling and cursing, bleary-eyed and groping, they climbed into their togs and trickled desultorily down to the big mess-hut.

Panhandle went to Big Tom's cabin and knocked. He received no answer. He opened the door gently and peered in. Fully clothed except for his hat and boots Big Tom lay spread-eagled on the top of the bunk. His eyes were screwed up, his mouth open; he breathed heavily, his face was flushed. Beside his bunk lay an empty bottle.

Panhandle wagged his head from side to side. He could never remember the boss being like that before. He could stand an enormous quantity of liquor. He knew his own capacity and never went above it. He'd evidently dived right over this time. Conscience? Maybe! Could a ruthless killer like that have a conscience? Panhandle closed the door softly again and walked away.

It was almost noon when Big Tom appeared. He was spruced-up but looked a little fuddled and choleric. He saw Mack and made for him. Mack slid away and sought refuge once more in the cookhouse. Big Tom went to Johnny Logan and Johnny began to pass word round the camp. The share-out from the bank job was to be held in the mess-hut pronto!

The men knew that this would be done on the usual principle. The men who had actually done the job would, naturally, get the biggest share. All the others would get smaller equal proportions, except old Panhandle and Johnny Lee, the cook, who were paid regular wages.

The boys who did the bank-job were due for a rest now. They wouldn't be going on the next one or two raids unless they were very big ones, rustling or such-like. Next time another bunch would be the ones to have the biggest cut. It was fair. Things broke pretty evenly for everybody, Big Tom made sure of that. It was unusual for him to have a share-out immediately after the job. Still, nobody was going to belly-ache about that ....

As they trooped into the mess-hut the leader was already there, seated at the edge of the long table which Johnny Lee had just freshly scrubbed. At his elbow Tom had a bulging saddle-bag and a small fat leather sack. He did not speak to anybody but watched them file in, his heavy-lidded eyes sombre, his face hard. The men who had been on the actual raid seated themselves nearest to him.

Finally, when every seat around the table was occupied and also the benches along the wall, Big Tom said: 'Is everybody here?'

'Yeh – Yeh.'

'If anybody's missing somebody else 'ull get their share. An' that's their lookout .... Who's on guard next?'

Four men rose. Big Tom gave them a bundle of notes each. 'Git goin',' he said. 'Send the other four down here, pronto!'

The men filed out. Tom tipped the bags up. All greenbacks. Done up into neat little piles tied with tape. Evidently the Lobo leader hadn't been idle this morning.

Tom separated the four biggest packs from the rest. There were five of them.

'Johnny,' he said. Logan caught the bundle which was tossed to him. 'Hank! Chequa! Pete! Mack!'

They all took their bundles except the last-named, the lean, yellow-headed kid. He stood up and shoved the pile back with the rest.

'I don't want it, boss.'

Big Tom rose, too, his eyes startled, his face had gone suddenly drawn and pale.

'Why not?'

'Cos I figure some of it's blood money. There should be another man here gettin' a cut. He ain't. I figure that sort of balls things up. I want no part of it.'

Big Tom's eyes blazed. He stepped back a little. The lean kid and the big man faced each other across the table. The latter's hands dangled near the butts of his guns. The younger's hands were on the table top, his thighs close to them, he was leaning forward staring at the other. His face was pale and drawn too. It was too late to back down now. Chairs scraped as men moved away from the table.

The two men stared at each other, thru' each other. Big Tom was the first to drop his eyes. Everybody tensed as he moved. But he raised his hands, put them both on the table too. With one he took up the bundle of notes Mack had refused.

Behind him was the pot-bellied stove. He turned and lifted the lid. He dropped the notes into the heart of the fire. Nobody spoke or moved. He turned again and looked at Mack. His face expressionless, his eyes cold.

'All right, Mack,' he said. 'I'm not goin' to fight with my right hand man. You got a lot to learn yet.'

Bewilderment showed on most faces. Mack straightened up. His tenseness left him but he seemed a little dazed. He shrugged his shoulders slightly, turned on his heels and walked out of the hut.

# CHAPTER THREE

More and more of late the Loboes were saying that their leader sometimes acted like a crazy man. Fancy burning good money because it had been refused by a cocky kid who wasn't dry behind the ears yet – no matter how good a gunny he was. The kid who Big Tom had taken in too, a starved brat, and looked after him and taught him to shoot, like he was his own son. A kid who seemed to be walking around most of the time now with a chip on his shoulder, mean as a sidewinder.

Mack didn't go out on the next two raids. Big Tom took one bunch out himself, then on the second job his place was taken by Johnny Logan. Evidently the Lobo leader wasn't meaning to use his 'right-hand man' yet awhile. But the younker didn't seem bothered none. He moped around the camp, scowling most of the time, saying little to anybody except Johnny Lee and old Panhandle.

After the two raids, both small but successful, the Loboes rested on their laurels. Quite a sizeable bunch of them went out on a spree. They invited Mack along but he declined. Nevertheless about an hour after they had swept out of the valley he saddled up his horse and rode out alone.

Big Tom watched him go. He turned to a man nearby, a dour redhead known solely as Jingo.

'Follow him,' he said. 'See where he goes, what he does. Don't let him see you unless you have to. If he gets in trouble help him out.'

'Sure, boss.' Jingo saddled up and followed in the wake of Mack. He wasn't much older than the kid himself. Twenty-four maybe. He was homely looking, his face was freckled, his red hair usually tousled. He spoke little but was pretty-well liked. He looked like any other happy-go-lucky, shabby cowboy. Nobody would've taken him for a hardened owl-hooter.

So often was the tragedy of these lawless Western days: a young cowboy, a kid who back East in better circumstances would still be going to school, took to the owlhoot trail for excitement. For a bit he might have easy pickings then one day he'd get in a fix, have to shoot his way out. Kill a couple of men. Pretty soon killing men came pretty easy to him. He was a faster and better shot than people he came up against because he had trained himself to be, that was the way he lived. And so it went on – until one day he tangled with one of his own kind – and that was it. He went out in smoke. A blaze of glory. Another bit of the old West shot away into eternity.

Big Tom had said: 'A gunman keeps running into people who are jealous – who think they're faster than he is. The best thing he can do is just avoid 'em. Unless he's sure. Still, no matter how fast you are there's always somebody who can beat you. It goes like that, right the way up to Ben Thompson and John Wesley Hardin and,' with a crooked smile 'even Big Tom Heineman .... If it's forced on you, wal, there's nothin' else for it. Keep cool, watch the other man's eyes not his hands. That way you can tell when a man's gonna draw even before he moves a muscle. The cold, careful man always lives the longest – if he's fast too ....'

37

Nobody would've taken Mack Danvers for an owl-hooter either. He was lean and hard-looking. He didn't look like a kid you could meddle with. But he didn't look shifty or vicious. His mouth and chin were firm, there was a direct look about his blue eyes and altho' they were kind of hard and cold most of the time, they lit up when he smiled. Cocky and pugnacious, but to an outsider he looked a fairly likeable young cuss.

It was kind of foolish for him to go back to San Antonio so soon after the furore Tom and he had created with the help of the gambling gents and the two rangers, but Mack didn't stop to think about that. He had liked the look of the Latin-American border town. During his last visit he hadn't seen much of it, he hadn't been there long enough, so he decided to pick up where he left off. And this time alone. Which was most foolish. If he had been a seasoned outlaw he wouldn't have dreamed of going near the place for about twelve months – particularly after tangling with the Texas Rangers, who had a post right there in the town.

He did have enough sense to bed his horse down at a different livery-stable; and gave a wide berth to the saloon where he'd had a run-in with the gamblers. It was twilight, a quiet time, mealtime for most folks. Mack had a real he-man feed at a chow-house close to the stables where he had left his mount. Nobody paid any attention to him. He was just another saddle-tramp, just another customer. He looked like a gunny, a two-fanged gunny at that. But San Antonio was full of 'em. A dime a dozen they were. As long as they didn't start shooting each other nobody bothered about them. Mack relaxed and rolled himself a quirly. With good chow and strong coffee under his belt he felt easier in mind. The depression that had encompassed him had lifted. He felt almost lit up. He remembered the gaming he had done last time he was here. He had plenty of cash; too much, he hadn't spent any of it. Why not go out and buck that ol' tiger once more?

Still he did not make a move but sat relaxed, smoking, gazing around him. It was kind of pleasant in here, in this long low, dusky room lit by swinging oil lanterns which were a constant menace to over-tall men. A faint blue haze of smoke hung from the ceiling, drifted around the lanterns, it shifted more swiftly when the doors opened and shut, and the lanterns swung gently. The smell of food was thick upon the air, but the place was clean – as such places went. It was popular too and rapidly filling up. A big black-bearded workman took the chair opposite Mack. Finally the younker rose to make way for somebody else and meandered outside.

The streets now were full of lights, tho' there was very little actual lighting in them: illumination streamed from the uncurtained windows each side. From the saloons, the dance-halls, the gambling houses, and even the brothels – only *their* back and upstairs windows were heavily curtained. As Mack paced nonchalantly along the sidewalk a painted hussy came out of one of these place and caught his arm.

Looking down at her he was surprised, almost shocked to see that she was only a kid, little more than fourteen or fifteen. He'd never had any truck with women of any kind. He felt pity and a slight loathing for this one. She was thin and kind of pretty but her face was raddled, old before its time.

'Come on in, cowboy,' she said huskily. 'It's a big night tonight. Let me show you, cowboy.'

'Sorry, chiquita,' he said, trying to disengage his arm. 'I've got an appointment with a man.'

She still clung to him, pressing her body against his.

She looked around her, such soliciting was frowned upon even in San Antonio.

'Come on, cowboy,' she said. 'Have a drink with me. It's on the house tonight.'

Mack's good-humour left him suddenly, she was getting on his nerves. 'Cain't be done, chiquita,' he said. But she was pulling him. Despite himself he was going with her. He'd never been inside one of these places. Men and guns were all he knew … But, what the hell! that was all he wanted to know. Big Tom was right about women (he had done his work well).

'Let go of me,' said Mack.

'Aw, come on,' said the girl.

Mack raised his free hand and slapped her hard across the face. She spun away from him, back against the frame wall beside the door of her abode. Her arms were spread out against the wall, her hands clutching like talons as she straightened herself up. Her face was dead-white, drawn in the light that streamed from the windows. Her eyes blazed, a thin trickle of blood ran from her mouth.

'You bastard!' she said.

Then she turned and went thru' the door. It swung-to behind her.

Mack turned sharply to almost collide with a man, a plump *hombre* in black street clothes with a cigar stuck in the middle of his fleshy face.

'I didn't like that, young man,' said the plump hombre.

'Fine town yuh got here,' said Mack. 'When gels come out intuh the street and claw at people.'

The plump man took his cigar from his mouth and said: 'Daisy was a mite hasty I'll admit. She's young and impetuous. But there was no call to hit her.'

A sudden feeling came over Mack, a wolfish feeling; he

wanted to kill the plump *hombre*.

'So,' he said, 'Are you aiming to do anythin' about it?'
He stepped back a little, measuring his opponent. He was
ice-cold, careful: the inherent qualities of a born
gunfighter. He noted that the other wore a pearl-handled
gun, the butt protruded from the open wings of his
cutaway coat. It wasn't there for ornament, it was in position for a quick draw. He looked up into the plump
*hombre*'s eyes, small, dark, pouched, glittering in the lamplight.

Two more men were coming along the boardwalk,
another man was standing in an open doorway, how long
he had been there Mack did not know. Altho' he saw all
this he still watched the man in front of him, those eyes.
The eyes crinkled, the plump man smiled.

'Forget it son,' he said. 'I've never fought over a woman
yet and I ain't aiming to. Not as I wouldn't like to try you.
Maybe we'll meet again.'

He tipped his black sombrero and came forward. Almost
mechanically Mack stepped aside to let him pass. Then he
continued on his own way. The man in the doorway spoke
as Mack passed. 'D'yuh know who that is, mister?'

Mack stopped. 'Nope.'

'That's John M. Madin.'

Mack was surprised. John M. Madin, notorious gambler
and premier among gunmen. That fat *hombre*!

'No,' he said, feigning nonchalance.

'You wuz lucky,' said the man in the doorway. He spat
reflectively, then left his post and stepped inside.

Mack walked on. The man had said he was lucky; Madin
was the deadliest gunman in this territory, miraculously fast
they said. Was he lucky, Mack wondered? *He* was fast too. A
man's reputation rested on the people he had beaten to

the draw not those he hadn't. Everybody had a master somewhere. Was it not possible that he, lean, muscular, cool, was a match for that suave, pot-bellied *hombre*. Then he suddenly remembered the things Big Tom had told him; he was beginning to think the way all gunmen thought sooner or later, that he was faster than any of 'em, and even wanting to put it into practise, too. Even tho' he now knew the identity of the plump *hombre* he still wished that Madin had throwed down on him. He smiled cynically as he walked. If he had fought maybe the things that had been puzzling him of late wouldn't be puzzling him anymore .... Or maybe Madin would've met his master.

Mack dismissed the subject from his mind as he turned into a small honky-tonk. He'd get himself a bellyful of liquor, then he'd have a flutter. And no more women. Big Tom was right. They were plumb pizen. A man did much better to rely on his two guns and his speed on the draw. He went up to the small bar and ordered himself a rye. He took it from the plump, sweating bartender and turning, with one foot on the brass rail, nonchalantly surveyed the room. But quickly in case his old friends the gamblers or those two rangers were anywhere around. Maybe they wouldn't recognise him anyway with his hat slouched over his eyes and the thin moustache he was growing on his upper lip. It promised to be a luxuriant yellow growth – they were the fashion nowadays. It would make him look older and serve as a disguise. He could whip it off any time he pleased.

He spotted a faro layout in a corner. Over there 'the tiger' was being 'bucked' by quite a bunch of enthusiasts. The dealer and his pard were strangers to Mack. He figured his feet would lead him there when he'd had some more liquor. He turned back to the bar.

'Gimme the bottle, Joe,' he said. The bartender

grinned greasily as he shoved the bottle across and took Mack's greenback. 'Call me Cal,' he said.

'Right, Cal, have one with me.'

'Thanks.'

Cal had more than one with him. He knew how to kid the customers along. Besides he had taken quite a liking to this lean kid who, as he drank, got more friendly and garrulous – but, with native caution, wasn't drunk enough to utter anything but mere banalities. As for Cal, he was a past master in the art of small talk, nobody got anything out of him. And as for being boozed, he could drink a barrel without much effect. Unless the boss caught him at it.

*He very nearly did.* Cal muttered an excuse me and went, with alacrity, to serve somebody else. A voice behind Mack said: 'We meet again, pardner.'

The young man turned his head. Beaming at him was John M. Madin.

'Hullo,' said Mack. 'Didn't 'spect to see you again.'

'This is my place,' said Madin with a flourish of his plump hand.

'You don't say. Have a drink then.'

'Thanks I will.' Madin took the bottle and poured himself one. 'I own a few little places around here.'

'You don't say,' said Mack again. He was joshing the other man, but in a friendly-like way.

Madin beamed again, he didn't look at all like the dangerous gunfighter he was reputed to be. He shook the bottle. It was nearly empty. He poured himself and Mack another one apiece, then he called Cal.

The barman bustled up. 'Yeh, boss.'

'Bring another bottle.'

'Sure, boss.'

'This is on the house,' said Madin.

Mack grinned. 'Thanks. But I couldn't drink another half-bottle with yuh. I've had plenty now.'

'Have a few anyway,' said Madin. He'd obviously had pretty well himself. Probably in one of his other 'little places'. He was in a generous amicable mood. But he could still be dangerous. Men with liquor in them are moody, easily antagonized. Mack felt amiable too. He meant to humour Madin. He didn't want to upset him and maybe start something, particularly right here in the gunman-gambler's own 'little place' where he'd have boys at his beck and call.

The plump man opened the bottle and refilled both tumblers. They clinked glasses.

'I like you, young man,' said Madin owlishly. 'You got sense. You don't scare easily.'

'You're a mighty fine feller yourself, Mr Madin,' said Mack.

'You know who I am.'

'Yeh.'

Madin beamed again. 'Ain't you scared I might drill yuh?'

'I don't think you'd do that,' said Mack.

For a moment the older gunman's eyes had a calculating look as he sized up this double-fanged youngster. Then he beamed again.' No, I don't expect I would.'

But Mack wasn't fooled. Madin wasn't all that drunk. He probably never was and, living as he did, could probably be ice-cold, ready for action in a second. Madin's tipsiness was just his hail-fellow-well-met saloonkeeper's pose.

Mack tipped his glass. Then he stiffened. He hoped the sudden shock did not show in his face. Coming along the bar was a very tall, lean man with a long, newly-healed scar down the side of his face. Mack recognised him instantly. It was the ranger called Bob with whom Big Tom and he had a run-in last time they were in San Antonio. Big Tom had given the man that terrible, mutilating scar. Bob had seen Mack but no sign of recognition showed in his face … still, the light had been poor in the livery-stable that night.

Madin turned and saw the newcomer. 'Howdy, Bob,' he said. 'Have a drink with me an' my young friend here.'

'Thanks, John,' Bob nodded to Mack. Mack grinned back at him.

'Let me introduce you two,' said Madin. Then his plump face puckered. He turned to Mack. 'What did you say your name was?'

'Carter,' said Mack quickly. 'Jim Carter.'

Madin beamed again. 'Mr Jim Carter, meet Mr Bob Laight.' The two men shook hands.

Mack's mind was set at rest. The ranger did not recognise him. The three men drank together.

'Kind of quiet in town lately, Bob,' said Madin.

'Yeh, quite a Sunday-school atmosphere.' The ranger grinned. Bob almost winced. The grin gave Bob's face, with that terrible scar a hideous look. The picture flashed thru' Mack's mind of Big Tom's descending flashing gun and the blood gushing from the lean man's face. Before that Bob hadn't been a bad-looking fellow. Big Tom was the one Bob would remember, he was easily remembered. By this time the ranger had probably forgotten all about the big man's companion.

Mack decided to play things along as he had planned. After a bit he said: 'I think I've had enough liquor for a while. I came in here in the first place to have a crack at the ol' tiger. I think I'll go over there while I can still see his spots.'

Madin and the ranger both laughed uproariously. 'See yuh later,' said Mack with a flip of his hand, and he left them.

'So long Jim,' Madin called after him.

He joined up with the faro-layout in the corner. But his mind wasn't on the game. He lost pretty heavily. Finally he decided to go outside for a smoke. Maybe he'd leave town after all just to be on the safe side. As he left the saloon Madin and Bob were still talking at the bar. They didn't look in his direction.

As Mack passed thru' the batwings and on to the sidewalk he did not see the man who darted suddenly into the shadows around the corner of the building.

Mack produced the 'makings', rolled himself a quirly and lit up. He moved away from the lighted window of the saloon and leaned against a hitching post on the corner where the sidewalk broke and there was a narrow dark alley. The breeze here, blowing thru' the gap from the open land behind, was cool and sweet after the close smoke-laden atmosphere of the saloon. Mack's quirly drawed well. He smoked reflectively. He was on the opposite corner from the man in the shadows tho' he did not know that. The watcher, peeping from his hiding-place, could see the red glow of his quarry's cigarette. He waited.

He had not had long to wait for Mack suddenly stiffened and dropped his smoke. His hand reached for his gun.

'Hold it!' rapped a voice. 'Up with 'em.' It was the voice of Bob, the ranger. He came out of the blackness of the alley, a dim, hardly tangible form. Mack knew he was a perfect target there on the corner. He slowly lifted his hands.

'What's the idea?' he said.

Bob came a little nearer. Mack could see the glint of the gun in his hand, the blurred outline of his form behind it.

He calculated his chances and decided they were nil. You just did not take such chances with a trigger-happy Texas Ranger.

'Didn't think I'd recognised yuh did yuh, *hombre*?' said Bob. 'I don't forget easily. This time you are comin' along to the post with me. An' if you try any funny business I'm gonna kill yuh.'

'You're crazy,' said Mack. 'I don't know what you're talkin' about. I only jest rode in town. I don't know who you are …. But I'd like to know what your game is!' he finished hotly.

'You're jest wastin' your breath by tryin' tuh bluff,' Bob told him. 'Move along. Go on. That way,' he jerked the gun.

Mack stepped from the sidewalk on to the street, moved along slowly. Then it happened. A boot slapped on the boardwalk, flame stabbed the shadows. Bob spun around, hit in the shoulder. He dropped on one knee. A man came along in a crouch, as he passed the lighted window Mack saw his face. It was the red-headed Lobo, Jingo. He was fanning his gun. Bob had thrown himself flat, triggering desperately. The stream of hot lead went over him.

Jingo had been hit too, he staggered, his gunhand lowering. Even as Mack drew, Jingo fired again. The ranger's face, full in the lamplight, dissolved in blood. Then it hit the boards and was hidden and still.

Mack reholstered his unfired gun. His head was spinning with the swiftness of it all. He ran to Jingo. Even as he reached him the redhead crumpled up in a tight ball on the sidewalk. He jerked once and lay still. Mack bent over him, straightened swiftly. He knew death when he saw it. *Two of 'em.* Voices bawled. Feet thudded inside the saloon. The customers were waking up. Mack ran for the nearest horse.

A man came thru' the saloon doors. Mack turned. It was Madin. Both men simultaneously slapped leather. Madin's guns were half out of their sheaths when both Mack's slugs hit him. Little puffs of smoke started from his clothes. He hit the doorjamb with his shoulder, bounced from it, and sprawled full-length beside the body of young Jingo.

Mack was already in the saddle. He tore the reins free from the hitching post, and thumped the beast with his heels. He turned, smashing the saloon windows with a blatter of shots. Then he was low over the horse's back, riding at breakneck speed out of San Antonio. Wild exultation surged within him. He had beaten John M. Madin to the draw!

It was dark early morning when he reached the hideout. The guards challenged him, then let him thru'. He rode up to Big Tom's cabin and dismounted. The light was on. The door was flung open. The Lobo leader was framed there, a gun in his fist, his mop of hair tousled on his leonine head.

'Mack?' he said.

'Yeh.' Mack strode towards him.

Big Tom stepped aside and let him into the cabin. 'Have you been followed?' he snarled.

'Nope. I had a start. Nary a sign of anybody.'

'Trouble again?'

'Yeh. Jingo's dead.'

Big Tom put the gun on the deal table and sat down on the edge of his bunk. 'How?'

'Shootin',' said Mack tersely. 'I wouldn't be here if it wasn't for him. Good thing you sent him to foller me after all.'

This was a double-edged remark but Big Tom ignored it. He said:

'Where did it happen?'

'San Antonio.'

This time the Lobo leader bounded to his feet. 'You crazy young fool! Hadn't yuh any more sense than to go there after the ruckus we had?'

'I made a helluva mistake. I admit it.'

'You admit it,' snarled Tom. 'But that don't bring Jingo back does it?' Then he sat down again suddenly. A queer smile crossed his lips. 'I guess that puts us square,' he said almost to himself.

'I'm mighty sorry about Jingo,' said Mack. 'I guess he saved my bacon.' He turned to go.

'Sit down,' said Tom. 'Tell me how it happened.'

Mack turned back and sat on the edge of the table. He told his tale in a hard, studiedly unemotional voice – altho' he could still see everything vividly before him.

Tom was unemotional too. When Mack had finished that queer smile crossed his face once more. 'So John M. Madin throwed-down on you and you beat him to it.'

'Yeh. Don't you believe it?'

'Yes, son, I believe it,' said the Lobo leader. 'You could beat anybody in this territory now. You're a born gunfighter. You could even beat me I guess.' He shrugged his shoulders and gave a little spurt of harsh laughter. 'I never had such a good pupil.'

When Mack left him he was still sitting on the edge of his bunk. But as he was making for the bunkhouse the cabin door opened again and Big Tom called him.

He turned back. 'Yeh?'

The Lobo leader said: 'You'd better lay low for a bit an' let that face fungus o' yours grow. I shall want you for a big job in a week's time.'

'All right.'

49

# CHAPTER FOUR

'Where are we now, Johnny?' said Mack.

Johnny Logan stared moodily out of the train-window.

'We're moving out o' the Pecos now,' he said. 'Next main stop El Paso. The boss's leaving things kinda late. D'yuh think anything's gone wrong?'

'Naw,' said Mack. 'I guess he's got his reasons.'

His voice was edged with asperity. Logan had done nothing but moan since they got on the train. Mack wished the Lobo chief had teamed him up with somebody else. He knew Logan hated his guts and he didn't trust him.

He looked along the coach. He knew there were fourteen of them altogether and in each were two or three members of the Loboes. Big Tom with three more men was right up the front. It was his job to stop the train. That would be the signal for everybody else to get moving. Mack and Johnny had their own particular job. Perhaps the most important one of the lot.

They were both smartly dressed in black broadcloth. Their guns were hidden by the tails of their coats. Mack's whiskers had grown to a luxuriant, blond growth. They made him look older, but less ornery, or so the boys said when they chaffed him. Johnny's clean-shaven, Indian-like features were inscrutable. The two of them looked like Western business men, or top-line gamblers. They were in the back seat. The one opposite them was empty.

A couple of seats away from them sat two more personages very similarly dressed. Both, however, were older men. The one was fat, Jewish-looking. He was Jonathon Ammons, vice-president of the Southern Pacific line. The other: big, brawny, hard-looking, was his personal and official bodyguard, a fast-shooting, brawling sidewinder known as 'Dead-eye' Pilson. On the seat at Pilson's elbow was a black leather bag. It was full of money. A payroll for railwaymen who were laying a branch line just outside El Paso. Or so Big Tom said. Where he had his information from no one knew. But it would be right. He had never failed to be right yet.

There were plenty other personages on the train. Railwaymen bound for El Paso. There was going to be a jamboree there to commemorate something or other. Bound to be lots more cash on the train. Even if there wasn't the bag Dead-eye Pilson guarded would more than compensate for the 'trouble' the Loboes must take. But there was a snag. At least, a snag from Mack and Johnny's point of view .... There were a couple or three more guards in this coach....

There were only seven more people in the coach besides Ammons and his bodyguard. There was nothing distinguished looking or rakish about any of them. Their faces were all cast in the same hard Western mould. It was their eyes and their movements that Mack watched. He had plenty of time to do so in this long train ride.

Finally he was pretty certain of the identity of two of the guards. They were young, fit-looking men. Their demeanour was tense and wary most of the time. Their eyes were hooded but they were quick to glance up if anybody moved. They sat across the opposite side of the aisle from Ammons and Dead-eye, and paid no attention to them. It seemed to Mack that their indifference in that direction was too studied. If there was another guard in this coach he hadn't spotted him yet. He told Logan of his conclusions. The other Lobo nodded surlily and hadn't argued about them.

A little later he said 'You get Dead-eye first. I'll watch them two ginks.'

'You know what Tom said,' Mack muttered. 'No shootin' if we can help it. Might start a panic an' ball everything up.'

'I've bin on train-jobs before,' Logan told him curtly.

Which means I ain't, reflected Mack sardonically. One score tuh the boy!

The country was beginning to bear a more fried-up aspect with every mile they passed along. Patches of sand, rock and scrub interspersed with brownish grassland. Then they passed between sandstone bluffs and suddenly the train pulled up with a jerk, throwing people forward in their seats. Johnny and Mack had been waiting for it for the last half-hour or so but it jolted them a mite.

In a trice Mack regained his balance and jumped into the aisle with both his guns drawn.

'Hi'st 'em!' he barked. 'All of yuh!'

Johnny Logan's Colt boomed in his ear and one of the guards, who had foolishly reached for his gun, slumped forward with a bullet in his head. Everybody else's hands shot up double quick, Dead-eye Pilson's among them.

'Stand up, all of yuh,' said Mack.

They did so. Ammons spoke up, his voice trembling.

'I'm vice-president of this line. I'll see ....'

'I know who you are,' snapped Mack. 'I ain't scared none. Keep your mouth shut an' your hands in the air. You saw what happened to your boy there,' he jerked his head in the direction of the dead man.

Johnny Logan joined Mack in the aisle. He had holstered one of the guns. He went along the car relieving each man of his weapons. He took the black leather bag from beside Dead-eye Pilson. The bodyguard scowled, his fingers, held high, twitched. Logan hit him a sudden back-hand blow with the barrel of the gun. He gave an agonized grunt and tumbled against his boss. Ammons squealed, his little eyes popping as he watched the unconscious gunman crumple at his feet.

'Watch yourself, pop,' said Logan sardonically. He put the black bag beside Mack, on the seat by the door.

Mack said: 'I'd like every gentleman here who's coat isn't open to reach across with his left hand and open it. Easy does it. My pardner's comin' round now to relieve you of any cash or valuables you may have. Also your weapons. As you've seen, he's mighty jumpy, I should advise you to play right along with him.'

'You talk too much,' said Logan out of the corner of his mouth. There was a sardonic gleam in his eyes. Mack shut up. Another score tuh the boy!

They'd got to get moving. Their time was nearly up. They ought to be jumping for it with the rest any minute now.

Logan had taken a canvas gunny-sack from his belt. He collected wallets, watches, rings, gold and silver cigarette cases. The passengers were a rich bunch. Even the other guard, the only one left on his feet, coughed-up a heavy silver time piece and a bulging billfold. He was mighty careful about it too; he didn't want to share the fate of his pard, who lay at his feet in a rapidly widening pool of blood. Logan whipped guns from the people too, throwing them immediately thru' the open windows. Looking around the carriage Mack reflected there had only been three guards altogether, counting Dead-eye, after all. Johnny and he had figured there might be more. Besides the fat trembling vice-president, his unconscious body-guard, the dead man and his pard there were five more people. None of them looked like gunmen and they were mighty docile. A couple of 'em looked like they might faint any minute. One in particular, a wizened rat-faced runt who stood quite close to Mack was in an obvious state of collapse. His face was yellowish and he was trembling all over. His hand, held over his head, quivered like leaves in a strong wind.

Johnny Logan rejoined Mack. The latter barked: 'Keep your hands up, all of yuh. Now turn around!'

All the passengers shuffled around and turned their backs on the two bandits.

'Take the bags and go first,' hissed Mack. 'I'll be right behind yuh covering 'em.'

With a curt nod Logan holstered his gun and grabbed the leather bag and the gunny-sack. He slid back the door and stepped outside. Mack heard him open the outer door and hiss, 'All right. Get goin'.'

Mack said: 'No moves now unless you want me tuh start blastin'.'

He edged out thru' the sliding door, turned swiftly to the outer one. Out of the corner of his eye he saw a movement in the carriage. He turned, surprise flashing thru' his brain like a blinding light. The rat-faced runt's draw was a swift blur as he brought out a derringer from some hidden place in his breast. Before Mack's gun was half-round the little weapon barked. A blow in his side, a searing pain, knocked Mack sideways. The next slug whipped past his face. He triggered desperately. The runt threw himself flat on the floor. Mack turned and flung himself thru' the outer door. He hit the ground on all fours, pain almost blinding him.

'Johnny,' he called urgently.

But he might have saved his breath. Johnny wasn't bothering about Mack. He was already climbing, making for the bluffs. All along the line Loboes were leaving the train and running for the bluffs. Some of them turned to snap shots back at the carriages, keeping the passengers cowed.

Mack heard Big Tom bawl: 'Straight on across the sandstone. There're horses there.'

As usual the Lobo leader had planned things admirably and hadn't bothered to let anybody know about it. Maybe he didn't trust his own men enough. It was queer that such thoughts should flash thru' Mack's mind, at such a time, as, sweating with pain and effort he limped in the wake of Johnny Logan. He stopped thinking, only acting instinctively, as a shot whipped his hat off. He dived, rolling. He got a confused glimpse of a figure in the doorway of the carriage he had just quitted. Raising his elbow he fired back. The man dived out of sight. It was the runt.

What a cool actor the man was. He'd had 'em fooled. He was a little, sharpshooting coyote.

Mack began to run again, holding his side with one hand, his gun in the other. He ran crouching, veering from side to side. Slugs kicked up the dust in front of him.

Then a Colt boomed close by. It wasn't Logan, he was well in front. He didn't mean to come back and help his rival. It was another Lobo, an oldster known as Idaho.

He grabbed Mack by the arm. 'Come on younker.'

'Thanks, Idaho.'

The old man uttered a blustering curse and triggered again. 'Git back, you skunk!'

He half-pushed, half dragged Mack thru' a cleft in the sandstone. Into cover, and beyond, where the horses waited. He whipped a scarf round Mack's waist, pulling it cruelly tight. 'That'll hold yuh for a while,' he said.

'Tie him to a horse,' said Big Tom.

Idaho and another man tied Mack to a horse, his hands round the beast's neck, his feet under his belly. They didn't have time to be gentle and he passed out before they had finished.

The next thing he remembered was a jolting, stabbing nightmare, pincers tearing and gouging at his flesh, sickness which made his stomach writhe, blackness shot by spurts of blinding white light.

When things become a little clearer he realised it was night. The pungent smell of horseflesh was right beneath his nostrils, the horse's mane roughly tickled his ear and neck. The new unfamiliar sensation made him forget his pain for a second.

Then it returned again. All over him, but reaching its screaming, searing culmination in his right side. He tried to move his hand down there to feel the place, to press it, to try to ease the agony in some way. Then he realised his hands were tied round the horse's neck.

The wound felt sticky. It was probably bleeding again. He had an overmastering desire to find out, to investigate thoroughly. This grinding agony belonged to him, was part of him, but he could not even try to do anything about it. It was maddening having his hands tied like this, altho' he knew the boys had done it to prevent him tumbling from the saddle. His legs were tied too. But that wasn't so bad. He could put up with that.

Another horse moved nearer to his, detaching itself from the others that were already around, vague bulks with creaking leather and jingling spurs. The rider leaned over towards Mack.

'How yuh feelin', younker? I jest seen your head move. You've had quite a spell of shut-eye.'

'Can yuh reach over an' cut my hands free, Idaho?' said Mack. 'Maybe I won't feel so bad if I can have my hands free. I'll be all right.'

'Yuh sure?'

'Yeh, I guess I've still got enough grip left tuh keep me upright in a saddle.'

'All right.' A knife flashed in Idaho's fist as he bent nearer. Then Mack's hands were free. He flexed the fingers thankfully.

Idaho said: 'The boss's mighty concerned about yuh. But we gotta keep movin'. There's a posse on our tail, we figure they ain't so far away either.'

'Yeh,' said Mack 'Where are we?'

'Pecos,' said Idaho laconically. 'Still quite a way from home.'

The boundaries of the Pecos were not clearly defined, except by the river of that name which bounded it on one side. They still had plenty of riding to do. Well, Mack reflected sardonically, maybe if he got too big a burden Big Tom would finish him off like he'd done for Pinto Cabot. In time that seemed ages ago but for the young Lobo it was still a vivid memory.

He cautiously moved his arm, every movement caused him agony, and gingerly touched his side. The improvised

57

bandage was saturated with blood. Mack pressed his hand there gently. The blood didn't seem to be flowing very fast. Maybe he could staunch it even more. He pressed harder with the palm of his hand, encompassing the wound.

Sudden agony made him reel, waves of sickness buffeting him.

The voice of Idaho came faintly to him. 'You all right, younker?'

He felt himself nodding his head as if he would shake it off. He had let go of the reins but held desperately to the harsh thickness of the horse's mane.

He heard himself say harshly: 'Yeh, yeh. I'm all right.'

The sickness passed a little. A weak drowsiness overtook him. He wondered if he could hold out until they got to camp – if they ever got there. Perhaps it would be better to roll from the horse and lie down in the waving brown grass of the Pecos.

Maybe he would've done just that if his feet hadn't been tied. He rode with one hand pressed to his side. The other hand grabbed the reins again and was clinging. What kept him upright he did not know .... He was part of the horse, they were moving along, jog-jog, in a dream; a dark, never-ending half-nightmare....

This half-nightmare was at least better than the agony of full consciousness. The jog-jog suddenly ceased and the agony returned. The horse had instinctively halted as those around him did so. The pain buffeted Mack and beat him down. Mentally he was on his knees. The pain was so great that the sensation passed into numbness. It was a fresh experience in the gamut of those he had passed thro' in his nightmare ride. It didn't seem quite as bad as the others. He leaned forward drowsily on the horse's neck. They had stopped. He figured somebody would tell him why pretty soon. He wasn't bothered a lot .…

Then he heard the voice of Big Tom Heineman. It seemed to be booming in the distance, as if the Lobo leader was bawling down a tunnel.

The voice said: 'Listen .… Yuh can hear 'em. They're keepin' on our tail. We can't afford to lead 'em to the hide-out. The only thing we can do is stop an' fight. It's our only chance. Besides we've got a wounded man with us .…'

That's me, thought Mack foolishly. Maybe this is the payoff. And maybe not. He figured he could still shoot even if he was wounded.

Big Tom was saying: 'Up ahead is a small canyon. We'll hole up in there an' ambush 'em. Or at least most of us will. I want about four of yuh to keep on riding. Ride hard. Make a noise. Then they won't suspect. We'd better get movin' again now in case they find out we've stopped and get suspicious.'

The cavalcade jogged on. Ten minutes riding brought them to the canyon. The actual trail was narrow, bounded on both sides by outcrops of boulders, fantastically shaped, natural cover. Beyond these the sheer walls of the canyon swept upwards.

Big Tom led his men about halfway along the narrow rocky cleft then called a halt.

He ordered four men to keep going. They clattered on.

'Now get in cover each side of the trail. Keep your horses out o' sight. Most of yuh have got rifles. Wait till I fire the first shot then let 'em have it.'

Old Idaho moved alongside Mack.

'Cut my legs free, old-timer,' said the young man.

'You c'mon over in cover first.' The old Lobo led the two horses into the shelter of a huge lopsided lump of rock, a giant's plaything tossed there petulantly aeons ago.

Then he cut the bonds that held Mack's legs. The young man's body jerked, his legs were cramped, he swayed in the saddle.

With a hand on his shoulder Idaho steadied him.

'Thanks. I guess I'll be all right.'

The older man dismounted. Then he helped Mack slide from the saddle. After a lot of grunting, cursing, sweating, and stabs of pain, Mack finally got seated with his back against the rock and his rifle across his knees. He felt a whole lot better. He was even eagerly awaiting the fight. Even that was better than bouncing along at the mercy of a rough trail and a swaying hunk of horseflesh. Maybe he was gonna die anyway so if he stopped another bullet now to finish the job it would be a whole lot better than hanging around like a spavined heifer.

The murmur of men's voices had stopped now, the scraping of boots, the clanking of hoofs, the jingling of spurs and harness. The wind sighed, the sound of the four galloping riders came back with it. It seemed hardly credible that there was a party of men and horses in this narrow defile. But these men and horses were well-trained in stealth and silence.

Idaho stood by his own and Mack's mount, just in case, ready to grab their snouts if they decided to whinny.

'How're yuh feelin', Mack?' he whispered.

The young man gave a strained grin in the dark. 'Fine,' he said huskily.

Faintly on the breeze now came the steady drumming of the hoofs of the pursuers. Nearer and nearer they came until the metal was clinking on the hard rocks, the walls of the canyon throwing back the sounds hollowly. The horsemen slowed down, maybe they were wary. Maybe they were listening. The waiting men heard their voices. Then their

60

vague shapes loomed in view.

It was a thick atmosphere and the crack of Big Tom's Smith and Wesson cut thru' it like a razor-sharp knife. A man cursed in agony. A horse screamed in terror. Then the night was hideous with gunfire, booming, battering, screaming, tearing the darkness apart with light and sound. Nothing else existed but this battering, clattering, roaring din and the walls of the canyon took it up, bounced it back, threw it to the four winds in myriads of strange-sounding pieces. The noise seemed as tangible as the biting, searing red-hot lead.

The posse was thrown into terrible confusion. Many of them stopped bullets. When they finally found cover it was to leave five of their number lying motionless on the trail and another one crawling feebly. The Loboes opened up again. The man stopped crawling. Another deputy rose convulsively to his feet with a cry of agony then draped himself across the top of the rock which had been his shield.

The posse had now gotten organised. They began to retaliate. The Loboes hugged cover. Their billets were more solid and secure than the sparse cover which was all that was left for the posse further along the trail.

Big Tom was exultant as the enemies' bullets ricocheted harmlessly from the rocks and spent themselves out on the floor of the canyon. The wining echoes were like music.

'Give 'em hell!' he bawled.

Mack Danvers had fired his rifle with the very first volley. Whether he hit anything or not he did not know. His vision was impaired by a faint, smoke haze and the rifle felt like rubber in his hands. It bucked alarmingly, each jerk sending a lunge of red hot pain thru' the wounded side.

Mack gritted his teeth, hissing curses thru' them. The sweat globules starting on his forehead felt as big as marbles. He pressed the trigger mechanically, firing until the weapon was hot in his hands. He realised that it wasn't the rifle that felt rubbery but his own arms. The way he was shooting he was liable to hit one of his own pardners. He dropped the rifle with a weak curse and dragged out his Colt. The heavy boom of old Idaho's Sharps rifle echoed in his ears. He could hear the old man squealing and chattering like the old Indian fighter he was.

Mack hefted the Colt in his hand. It seemed a hell of a lot heavier than usual. His hand was trembling like a leaf. In this condition he'd have a job to hit a barn door at four paces. For all the good it was to him at present this forty-five might just as well be a hunk of old iron.

Like most gunmen when they are unarmed or when their weapons are of no use to them Mack felt a sudden surge of unreasoning panic. What chance would he have if these galoots got real close? He realised that despite his morbidly-cynical thoughts of a few moments ago, he still desperately wanted to live. Fit, cool, with two guns bucking in his deadly hands, he had been immortal. Now, sick and useless, he was already a beaten man.

# CHAPTER FIVE

The Loboes were picking their men now. Most of the posse were in very poor cover. Horses were being hit too. They were bigger targets. A couple of them bolted. The others milled around in terror, only the nearness of their masters preventing them from following the other two. Fighting men's horses, they were familiar with the sound of gunfire, but bullets whistling close, some of them finding a mark in quivering hide, was another matter altogether.

The posse was getting desperate. Finally they broke up, diving for their horses. Two of them were picked-off immediately. The rest mounted and got away at a frenzied gallop.

'After them!' bawled Big Tom, vaulting on to his own mount.

Whooping shrilly the Loboes set off in pursuit. Just outside the canyon a frenzied wounded horse was hobbling along. Its rider, one foot only in the stirrup, his body hanging, was humping along in its wake. His sightless eyes stared upwards at his slayers as they thundered past.

Old Idaho stayed behind in the canyon with Mack, who was lying on his back, breathing heavily, his eyes closed, his useless gun still held loosely in his hand.

He groaned as the oldster lifted him, but half-unconsciously tried to help as Idaho heaved him into the saddle of his horse and with lengths of rope, served him the same as on the beginning of the ride.

This done, Idaho gingerly felt the wound. Mack was too far gone to do little more than groan feebly. The scarf the old-timer had wrapped around Mack's middle was limp and soggy with blood but he did not dare remove it. Idaho took off the heavy plaid blanket-coat he invariably wore and stood in his shirtsleeves. He grabbed hold of the left sleeve and with a grunt tore it clean off. With this he wadded the wound again over the top of the scarf.

'I'll hafta have your bandanna, son,' he said and took it from around Mack's neck. He wrapped this round the young man's waist too and tied it tightly.

Mack came round, groaned and tried to sit up straight. Idaho lit a cigarette and put it between the younker's lips.

'That you Idaho?'

'Yeh, son. Rest easy.'

Mack dragged avidly at the quirly. 'Thanks,' he said. 'You're like a mother tuh me, old-timer....' Then he suddenly jerked his head, trying to gaze around him. 'What happened? Where are we?'

'The posse made a run for it. The boys're chasing 'em. They'll be back direckly.'

Hardly were the words bounced gently from the canyon wall and stilled, when the gang came clattering back. The two men heard Big Tom say: 'I guess they'll keep a-running. They ain't likely to come after us again until they get reinforcements. By that time we'll be at the hideout.'

The horses stepped gingerly around the bodies on the canyon floor. They were all erstwhile members of the ill-fated posse. Up till now the only casualty on the whole job was Mack. No wonder the leader was jubilant. He suddenly spotted the two in the shadows. His gun glinted in his hand. 'Who's that?'

'It's all right,' boss. It's me – Idaho. I've got young Mack here.'

The big man rode nearer. 'How is he?'

Mack spoke for himself. 'I'll be all right,' he growled. 'Let's git goin'.'

'All right! Let's ride.'

Dawn was pearling the sky and smearing it with streaks of red, an ominous sign, when the band were challenged by the guards who were mounted in cover beside the towering Ant Heap.

'All right, boys, it's us.' The Loboes filed into their domain.

The wounded warrior, a sorry specimen, was put in his bunk and lay like a wet rag. He breathed stentoriously with his mouth wide open. His face was unusually flushed and from time to time he tossed and moaned in fever.

Idaho fussed around him and presently was joined by Big Tom Heineman.

'We've got to get that slug out,' he said harshly. He took a sharp-pointed bowie-knife from the sheath at his belt and tested it with his thumb. 'Idaho, get me a bowl of boiling water and some clean towelling.'

'Right, boss.' Glad to be doing something practical, to be following decisive orders again, the oldster bustled off.

Mack lay on his back and opened his eyes slowly. He looked startled when he saw Big Tom standing over him with a knife, gleaming in the shadows, clutched in his fist. The Lobo leader's face was hard and shadowed, his eyes gleamed beneath the tangled, red mop of his hair.

'How'd' yuh feel, Mack?' he said.

The young man seemed to shake himself free from a trance. At length he said: 'Kinda weak I guess.'

'You've lost a lot of blood but we've got to get that slug out. Here, you'd better take a good shot o' this.'

He fished a flat bottle from his back pocket. He uncorked it and put it to Mack's lips. The younker held it and tipped it up. He took it away, coughing spasmodically. It was real raw stuff. It filled his belly and limbs with liquid fire. He felt better already. He took another swig.

Idaho entered with a bowl and a kettle. Over his arm was draped a strip of clean towelling. 'Piping hot right off the stove,' he said, putting down the kettle.

'Take another swig,' said Big Tom. Mack did so. 'Now give me the bottle and bite on this.' He shoved the whiskey cork between the younker's teeth. 'You're gonna need it,' he said as he began to unwind the bandages.

To Mack the next five minutes were blanketed by pain, fold after fold of it, as the Lobo leader gouged and probed.

But quite clearly Mack heard him cursing, heard him say: 'It's in mighty deep.' Then there was a particularly terrific burst of pain. Mack felt as if he was being pulled inside out and Big Tom's voice seemed far, far away as he said: 'Got the little critter. The water, Idaho, the towelling.'

Afterwards Mack had just enough strength left to croak: 'Thanks Tom.'

It was more than he had expected from the Lobo leader and he was duly grateful. Then the big man had gone and Idaho was just a hovering presence. The day passed and then night came again and Mack had an idea that all the boys including Panhandle and Johnny Lee, had been to see how he was faring. All of them came except Johnny Logan. Something told Mack that Johnny Logan hadn't been near. Maybe Johnny had hoped Mack would be dead meat by now. No fault of Johnny's if he wasn't. Mack made a point of trying to get well quickly now, if only to settle accounts with that treacherous sidewinder. That night a storm broke and raged for about six hours … and all that time Mack's fever ebbed and flowed, the pain came and went, he slept or tossed around in incoherent wakefulness.

The storm raged. The battle raged between Mack's system and the fever that strove to engulf it. His system was strong, ornery like its owner. Finally, like a bronc-buster wearing down a fiery mustang, Mack's inherent strength began to overcome the fever. Once cowed, it was quickly beaten entirely. After that Mack began to mend pretty quickly. The valley was silver with wetness and a watery sun.

After a while Mack could sit up and eat and drink voraciously. He learnt that his wound had been a mighty mean one, it could easily have proved fatal. Only Big Tom's prompt brutal handling had saved Mack's bacon.

Night after night now a card school gathered round Mack's bunk and he played with them into the small hours. He only saw Johnny Logan once and that was when the dark, lean man, who bunked in the other smaller cabin, came in to borrow a razor-strop because his own was cut to ribbons.

'Probably workin' his bile off on it,' said one of the men afterwards. 'He gets meaner and meaner. Pretty soon he's gonna fill himself so full o' pure pizen meanness that he'll bust, jest like one o' them snakes I've heard tell about they got in Arizony an' Mexico.'

The Loboes lounged and gambled and had spates of quarrelling. They took turns to go on the spree. A bunch of them pulled off a stage job but didn't get much out of it. Big Tom jeered at them for their failure. But he'd got nothing bigger lined up yet. He was marking time, waiting for some of the heat to cool off before he took the whole mob out again.

Mack Danvers was beginning to realise that he had something more than the health he was rebuilding, his keen eyes, lean, muscular body and pair of hands that were as swift and steady as ever. He also had a brain and a mind. He had been doing a lot of thinking of late. His mind went round and round in circles like a bull in a pen. He seemed to have aged tremendously in the last few months, more rapidly since he had been laid up.

Maybe the ageing process had a lot to do with his moustache, a lot of the boys had already gotten to calling him 'Granpaw!' Maybe he ought to shave it off. He guessed it would be safe to do that now; anyway, he'd take care not to go near San Antonio when he was round and about. He was getting more cautious, he was becoming an old hand, but he was still as sure of himself as ever.

The moustache had grown to a beautiful yellow walrus-type while he had been lazing around. It was even thicker than old Panhandle's and one or two of the boys had threatened to set fire to it. Mack decided to make a clean sweep and shave it all off. Have done with it entirely. He didn't want his venerable appearance to intimidate Johnny Logan any when it came to a showdown.

He got around the camp pretty well now but he had a limp which, tho' improving every day, probably would never wholly leave him. He played horseshoes behind the bunkhouse with the boys, helped his friends, Johnny Lee and Panhandle with the chores and spent hours sitting on a bluff with Idaho smoking and yarning.

One day the old owlhooter said a queer thing. 'This game's no good, Mack lad. Get hold of what you can and get out of it while you're young. I've been lucky. You've bin lucky so far but it mightn't last. Get out of it, move to some other territory, start legitimate. There's plenty of land down in the corner o' the Rio Grande jest cryin' out for younkers like you with a little mazama an' a whole lot of orneriness to come along an' claim a piece.'

Mack shrugged and spat and started talking about something else. But the old treadmill started up in his mind once more.

He did not see much of Big Tom and, when meeting both of them were mighty taciturn. Mack had to admit to himself that the Lobo leader was nursing him along. He did not send him on guard until he was almost as good as new again. Most of the time the big man seemed moody and preoccupied, inclined to scowl and snap peevishly if anybody spoke to him. Most of his men wisely left him alone.

From time to time he rode out on his lonesome, coming back late at night or early the following morning. The boys began to talk among themselves, to hint, with oblique references to inside information, which none of them had, that there was a big job in the offing. They were probably right anyway. They knew the signs.

Mack did not see much of Johnny Logan. He avoided the lean, dark, ranny, he didn't intend to show his hand till he knew he could back it up. Maybe Logan would start something first. He seemed to be studiously ignoring Mack but he always looked mean and savage as if some deadly poison was bottled-up inside him. The whole camp was aware of the antagonism between the two men. They

69

watched them both and waited for the brew to come to boiling point.

Mack had gotten more popular of late, he had staunch friends who would cheerfully riddle Logan if he tried to play it any way but dead straight.

Things came to a head suddenly in a very queer way. None of the rest of the Loboes ever discovered whether the incident was planned, spontaneous, or accidental. Only one man could tell them and he wouldn't ....

It was a clear, balmy morning. The kind of morning when all the little lizards came out of their holes and sunned themselves on the rocks, while their human counterparts, the Loboes, came out to make sport in the open air. Quite a school of them, including Mack Danvers, congregated behind the big bunkhouse and amused themselves with the time-honoured game of horseshoes. To toss a horseshoe and loop it around an iron spike in the ground from a dozen or so paces away seemed a childish way for grown men, hardened criminals all of them to boot, to disport themselves. But the game took skill and many of them were adept at it. They had plenty of practice. When they weren't shooting up the countryside, drinking liquor, mauling dance-hall girls or playing cards, this simple-looking game was their only means of amusement. It was their really harmless and healthy means of amusement. They gambled on it, and their oaths were vile and picturesque when they lost, their shouts loud and merry when they won.

Time and time again the horseshoes spun and flashed and bit the dust. Now and again they clanged against the iron spike and everybody cheered and slapped the skilful fellow on his shoulder.

Johnny Logan came around the bunkhouse into the

clearing where the dust shifted and was fine and trampled endlessly beneath heavy boots. Rather surprisingly, considering Mack was playing, Johnny joined the game. And his turn came right after his enemy's.

Each man fetched the horseshoes the previous player had tossed and took them back to the line to try his own skill. Johnny didn't seem keen to fetch Mack's shoes but he swallowed the nasty thing which had stuck in his craw, and scowling, played along. He was a more skilful player than Mack and, after a time, moved with alacrity to fetch the horseshoes, as if eager to prove his supremacy over his rival.

After one particularly poor effort of Mack's, Johnny permitted himself a smile as he almost bounded forward to retrieve the hoops. He was bending to gather them up when another horseshoe hit him full in the back of his neck, almost knocking him on his knees. He straightened, turning, his eyes blazing.

'Who threw that?'

'Sorry, Johnny,' said Mack, and he didn't sound that way at all. 'That wuz my last one. You moved in front a mite too quick that time.'

Logan's face whitened, he stood there with his hands dangling.

'You're sorry,' he sneered huskily. 'You took your time throwing that one didn't yuh? You meant it to hit me. Nobody does that to me ....'

'Hold it, Johnny!' The voice made him pause, his right hand a claw above the single gun tucked in his belt.

Idaho already had his gun out and it was pointing at Logan's middle.

'Cain't yuh see Mack ain't got a gun with him. You wouldn't shoot an unarmed man would yuh?' The oldster's voice was dryly cynical; he held no illusions about anything but he didn't intend to see his young pard shot down without having a chance.

'I'll fetch Mack's guns,' said one of the men.

'You can bring my gunbelt too,' said Logan with a sheer in his voice. 'We'll have this done proper.'

'All right.'

Even as the man left the group, Johnny Lee, who had watched everything thru' his cookhouse window, scuttled away, ran to Big Tom's cabin and began to hammer frantically on the door.

The man returned with the two gunbelts. The contestants buckled them about their slim waists. They were both very sure of themselves.

Watching Logan, Mack spoke up. 'Pity that little runt in the train didn't do the job for you, Johnny. He had a good try an' you let him. It wasn't your fault he didn't get me. He probably would've done if Idaho hadn't come along. I'm gonna kill yuh now so's we won't have to go on any more jobs together ....'

'Like I told yuh once before,' said Logan. 'You talk too much. Draw, man!' He crouched, thin lips stretching in a sneer, his eyes cold, watching Mack's face avidly. The latter noted that poise, watched those eyes and knew that here was no easy mark. Still John M. Madin hadn't been an easy mark .... Watch him, watch his eyes!

Time and silence hung in space and was brought rushing back to earth by a bull-like voice.

'Hold it. Up with your hands or you're both dead men.'

Big Tom confronted them with a Colt in each hand. There was no mistaking the hard killer's light in his choleric eyes. The two would-be contestants elevated their paws.

The Lobo leader said: 'I'll have no gunfightin' in this camp. Take their guns off 'em some of yuh.'

The two men were speedily relieved of their hardware. 'Now leave 'em be,' said Tom. The two men were left once more in their cleared arena. Without their fangs they looked kind of sheepish.

The leader turned to Mack. 'You fit enough tuh fight properly?' he said curtly.

'Yeh, I'm fit.'

'Strip tuh the waist then, both of yuh,' ordered the big man.

Idaho sidled along to Mack. 'You can't fight with that crack in your side, you'll bust it wide open.'

'It's all right,' said Mack. 'It's healed fine. C'mon help me get these duds off and quit worryin'. Maybe I'll git tuh kill him after all.'

Idaho shrugged and helped his young pardner off with his shirt and vest. If the crazy young fool wanted to bust himself up again that was his funeral. But something told him that even if Mack had been real sick he wouldn't have backed out after Big Tom had called him on.

'Yuh ready?' said the big Lobo.

Both men nodded. The leader shrugged and holstered his guns. The two men advanced on each other.

Mack wore a thick flannel body-belt around his waist, covering the sore scar of the wound in his side. It was completely healed. It irritated him a little at times, that was all. His body was lean and hard and perfectly hairless. The muscles rippled silkily beneath the skin as he moved. His shoulders were wide and sloping, stooping a little as if the weight of them and his broad chest made him top-heavy.

Johnny was lean too but more heavily built than Mack, blockier, more mature. His shoulders bulged squarely with

73

muscles, his body was wedge-shaped, tapering to a slim waist and a belly like a washboard. His skin was very dark and there was a curly fuzz of jet black hair over his chest. He too seemed a little top-heavy, advancing, catlike on the balls of his feet.

Then suddenly with startling rapidity he sprang.

Mack met his onslaught with his legs firmly apart, one foot a little in front of the other. Johnny's feet went slap-slap and the dust whirled. Mack caught his rapid blows on his shoulders and forearms, retaliating with a long right thrust that grazed Johnny's cheek, aiming the next one at his middle, trying to throw him off balance as he recovered from his dash. But Johnny was cat-footed, he swayed, covering his body with long hairy forearms, his face with balled brown fists.

The crowd came out of the trance after the gasp that had greeted Johnny's spring and shouted encouragement impartially to both men. Only Big Tom was silent and immobile, a cynical quirk to his lips.

The scuffed comfortable boots that the two men wore around camp slapped, thudded and scraped on the ground. The dust puffed and swirled about their ankles. The sound of fists meeting flesh was like the slap of an open palm on a steer's rump as the crowd became silent again. Already the paler body of the yellow-haired Mack was beginning to show fiery marks. The crowd 'hooed' and shifted as his fist snaked out and caught Johnny on the side of the head. The dark man staggered. Mack followed up, hitting out while the crowd yelled encouragement. But Johnny had covered up again, smothering the other's blows. He flung his fists apart. The right one buffeted Mack's shoulder, spinning him around .... Then they were toe-to-toe, hammering away at each other. They grunted as the blows thudded, and the crowd's yelling came in spates and murmurs.

Mack's fist rose and fell like a hammer, striking Johnny's neck. The dark man gave a choked grunt, his knees bent a little. Mack's left smashed through his guard and flush into his mouth. Johnny went down on his back, kicking his legs up and out as Mack advanced. Johnny rolled, landing on his feet instinctively, with catlike agility.

He crouched as Mack came on again; his lip was split, blood ran down his chin but, instinctively again, he side-stepped as Mack swung. The latter's fist flailed empty air. Johnny drove in, his bursted lips stretching in a snarl. He drove a fist into the pit of Mack's stomach. The yellow-haired man doubled-up. The crowd roared. Johnny's fists pumped mechanically like pistons. One of them hit Mack's lowering head. Everybody saw Johnny wince. But Mack felt it too. He was teetering, grabbing wind, and it bowled him over. He went down on his back.

Johnny's face was drawn and bloodied. He shook his bruised fist. Then his eyes blazed wickedly and he jumped. Mack rolled. Johnny hit the dust hard with both feet. Mack flung out his arms, grabbed, heaved. Johnny's legs were pulled from under him. The back of his head hit the ground before his body did. The crowd yelled and stamped.

# CHAPTER SIX

Mack flung himself across the intervening space and landed atop the dark man. Johnny flung out his legs, throwing Mack off. They clawed at each other like wildcats. Then they came to grips and rolled, locked together, each trying to get on top and stay there.

Mack gasped as Johnny squeezed his wounded side. He got his hands under the dark man's chin and pushed upwards with all his strength. Johnny continued to squeeze, but his eyes began to pop, sweat stood on his forehead as his head was forced slowly back. His grip slackened. Mack dropped his hands to the dark throat. Johnny hit him twice full in the face. Mack's hands were torn from his throat, leaving vivid red marks. The yellow-haired man's face gushed blood as he rolled away. The crowd roared.

Johnny sprang to his feet and, as Mack rose, brought both balled fists with terrific force up under his chin. Mack's feet left the ground. His knees went up as he rolled in the dust. Johnny was a bit too hasty flinging himself on top and received the knees in his stomach. He staggered away winded.

Mack was in even worse shape. He got on to his hands and knees, shaking his head from side to side like a dazed, wounded animal. He raised his head, his face was a bloody mess. He looked around for his foe, saw him and rose.

Johnny straightened, his breath coming in painful gusts.

They advanced on each other warily and circled, shuffling bearlike, their arms crooked, their heads sunk in their chests, their eyes hooded, looking for an opening. They gulped in air, scuffed their feet in the dust, biding their time while they strove to regain their strength and poise. They both looked sorry sights.

Mack was covered in blood and only recognisable by his bright yellow hair, although even the forelocks of that were stained with crimson. The gore was drying on his face giving it the awesome appearance of a painted Apache brave. His body was a curious piebald colour, red and white in patches. The body-belt at his middle was crumpled and dirty. His limping gait was very pronounced, he looked lopsided.

Johnny's lips were terribly swollen, they gave his lean dark face a bloated look. He looked cleaner than his opponent, but one of his eyes was half-closed. His black hair hung over his forehead in wet strands. He brushed it away from his eyes. His neck seemed to be bothering him a bit. He hung his head on one side in a queer way. His dark body did not reveal marks like his opponent's but at his shoulder a proud purple bruise was beginning to blossom. One leg of his trousers was torn almost from top to bottom.

The two men moved a little closer, pawing the air between them with clawed fists like feelers. The crowd murmured and waited following every movement with avid eyes, their heads waving to and fro like poppies in the breeze. Some of them stamped their feet impatiently and made passes in the air.

The two men watched each other's every move. Both top-line trigger men, they were very jumpy.

Johnny's puffed lips stretched in a travesty of a sneer. He feinted. Mack swayed and bobbed, grinning lopsidedly, painfully. Then their feet slapped hard in the dust as they came together suddenly. The crowd growled and shifted. Fists thudded on flesh once more and the crowd howled for blood.

The pace was slower, the fighting more calculated, there was much bobbing and weaving and feinting, and even a little wrestling. Passes and blows were cleverly avoided, blocked or parried. Neither of the men knew anything about pugilistic science. Their moves were the product of sharp wits and perfect muscular co-ordination. They were born fighting men – and mighty rough at that. There were no holds barred and neither of them hesitated in using everything they'd got if they had the chance.

Johnny chopped Mack sickeningly on the back of the neck as he bent from a body blow. Mack let his body sag and thrust his head forward blindly. It connected with the other man's dark face. Johnny's nose burst and splattered blood over both of them. The shock sent the dark man reeling while the blood ran down his chin and soaked his shirt-front. He shook his head and bright blobs stained the dark brown dust.

Mack bored in, flinging blows. Swaying from side to side, Johnny backed away. The yellow-haired man hit him twice more in the face before he began to take the blows on his shoulders and arms.

'Fight, Johnny, cain't yuh?' yelled somebody.

But Johnny *meant* to fight. He was no consistent back-pedal merchant. He had plenty of guts. But he was canny. Suddenly he swung a foot. His boot caught Mack on the kneecap. The latter's leg went from under him. He fell awkwardly on his side. Johnny spat blood at him and wiped his face with a loose, dangling sleeve. Then he threw himself at the fallen man.

Mack rose to his knees, striking out with a fist with the speed of a rattler. The blow caught Johnny low; everybody heard his agonized grunt. Then he landed on top of Mack and they were a threshing mass of arms and legs. Next thing, Johnny was flat on his back and Mack was on top of him, using his fists like hammers, beating at the other's face. Johnny's breath came in loud painful gasps. The blows maddened him. He yelled out like a man berserk and with superhuman strength arched his body, striking back at the same time with both fists at once. Mack was catapulted away from him and, as he went Johnny's boot caught him a crack on the chin, lending impetus to his flight.

Both men rose to their hands and knees, turning, on all fours, to face each other. They were down to the level of beasts now. And they acted that way. They advanced on all fours and sprang at each other. Tooth and nail, clawing, kicking, they rolled in the dust which rose in a little cloud around them.

The circle of spectators began to close in. Arms waved, hoarse voices yelled exhortations. Big Tom pushed his way to the front and stood with his thumbs tucked into his belt.

Mack was on top again, grinding a knee into Johnny's middle, his hands groping at the dark man's throat. Bloody murder glared in both their battered faces. They were no longer human; they had reverted to primeval beasts with the lust to kill the hated other beast.

Johnny's eyes were widening, glaring. His hands clasped at Mack's arms, drawing bloody lines on the flesh. His body arched, his face became contorted as the yellow-haired man's nails dug into his windpipe.

The dark man's hands reached higher, clutched the

breast of Mack's shirt. A terrible rasp came from his throat as he heaved. Mack was jerked forward. He fell on Johnny, almost smothering him. But his grasp on the dark man's throat had loosened. Johnny kicked frenziedly. Mack rolled clear, still striking out with fist and boot. For an incongruous moment they were both like infants lying side by side, pawing and kicking at each other. Then they both rose to their knees, grabbed and held on to each other. Still holding on, they got to their feet.

They were both weak. Their madness had subsided. But not their lust to kill. They broke away from each other. Then came in again. They stood toe-to-toe throwing punches, their tired bodies jerking with each effort, staggering at each blow. They grimaced at each other. Only their hate kept them going.

They got in closer until they were almost leaning on each other. Mack brought his knee up. Johnny grunted and jack-knifed. Mack hit him on the side of the head. Johnny went down, rolling feebly. Mack jumped on him, both his knees coming down with sickening force on the dark man's chest. Johnny gave a gasping cry, struck out frenziedly. A wild blow, delivered in agony and desperation caught Mack in the face. He was precipitated away and lay half-unconscious.

Johnny rose to his feet, clutching his chest. He staggered over to Mack and began to put his boot to the younger man's body. Three times he swung his boot, then with a strangled groan he crumpled up and fell face down across Mack's prostrate form.

The ring closed in. Both Idaho and Big Tom had their hands on their guns. The contestants were still.

Both of them were carted away to their bunks and there examined. Johnny's boot had opened up the wound in Mack's side. Mack's knees seemed to have busted a couple of Johnny's ribs. This was the main damage, the rest consisted of more easily-healed cuts and bruises.

Big Tom was savage. He wanted every available man for the big job that was in the offing. They had a fortnight in which to get well. Then they'd ride, like it or not. And they'd forget their differences for a bit or by God, he'd take them both on and tear them apart with his own two hands. The two younger men knew that their leader, huge brute-man as he was, could do this to them. They had time to reflect and their hate for each other became tempered with caution.

The days passed slowly. They both had to lay up for a while. Mack was first out. He lounged about the camp rather sheepishly. Despite the congratulations he received for the show he had put up against a hard case like Logan he felt rather deflated. His hate for the dark man was sullen now, it hardly smouldered. When Idaho said: 'Maybe it'd bin better if you'd killed him in the fust place,' he merely shrugged. It would've been better. Instead of it having to happen all over again. Maybe Logan would finish up by killing *him*. Mack wouldn't cork up any excitement about it either way.

He continued to practise his draw because it was now almost habit to do so. Every day he practised it. But he never fired his gun. Occasionally he saw Big Tom. Their greetings were brief and surly.

Mack learnt that Logan was up and out too. After that Idaho took to following the younker about like a pet dog. Mack figured maybe Big Tom had ordered the oldster to do so in case the two young men showed signs of tangling again. When he tried to pump Idaho the oldster was very noncommittal. Big Tom needn't have worried. The two men kept apart, only seeing each other at a distance, and then pretending they didn't. They both seemed to be biding their

81

time. Mack learnt that Logan was being watched too. It was lucky that they slept in different bunkhouses.

The valley drowsed in the sunshine. Time hung heavy on men who were used to action and excitement. Gambling, horseshoes, dice all got tame. After the fight such games were rather an anticlimax. More for sport and novelty than anything else the camp split themselves into rival factions: the Danvers men and the Logan men. They amused themselves by tossing fatuous remarks at each other, such as: 'My man's muscles are bigger'n your man's.' But nobody worked up enough meanness to fight over it and, after a while, the sport palled.

It drew nearer to the time of the big job. Though actually nobody knew the exact day or time. Except the boss of course and he was surly and uncommunicative, his usual pose at such times. It gave the men something to speculate and bet about. Also there was much cleaning and oiling of weapons, much grooming and re-shoeing of horses – as if they were going to a rodeo instead of a murderous, pillaging raid, and perhaps the death of any one of them.

Lowering clouds made the night black, the atmosphere heavy. From time to time a watery moon peeped through the clouds then, intimidated by the sight of such a melancholy vista, a slice of billowing, wind-blown range, disappeared again. The wind moaned as if born in the throes of torment. The night tossed and brooded on.

A large band of men rode steadily, silently, through it all The big man at their head was easily recognisable, even in the darkness. The lean man who rode at his side, sitting stiffly upright in the saddle, was Mack Danvers. At the other side of him, a bulky hunched figure who looked like a sack of wheat dumped in the saddle, was old Idaho. The rest of the band, in lines of three or four strung along behind them. Johnny Logan, strangely enough, was somewhere in the van.

The Loboes were a long way from home. They had ridden gently through the day. Then, at twilight, they camped in a small range of hills and had a meal of sandwiches and cold bottled coffee laced with rum, while they rested themselves and their beasts.

It was nearly midnight now and they rode steadily and purposefully, knowing they were near their destination. Nobody talked much. Big Tom was a good leader and at times such as this, the Loboes were like a small well-trained army.

The three men in the front, they had joined up on the last lap of the ride, had very little to say to each other. Surprisingly, it was Big Tom who, in a clear, disinterested voice suddenly tossed a slice of information to Mack Danvers.

'We're now riding into land belonging to the Loop W, one of the bigger spreads in Texas. It's owned by ol' Kit Maxton, he's a cripple, a mean, graspin' ol' goat; an' his daughter Judy. Judy was educated back East. I hear she's a reg'lar school-marm .... Right now, however, that don't concern us. What concerns us is that ol' Kit's got some of the slickest gunmen in Texas on his payroll an' his stuff's always heavily guarded. He's got one o' the biggest herds of longhorns an' Herefords in the State an' he don't like to lose a single dogie. He's never lost any yet – no ordinary cattle-snatcher 'ud risk ridin' 'em. There ain't a bunch of owlhooters around here who are strong enough. But Kit don't know about us. We've come a long ways. We take his men by surprise an' it's plain sailing – the finest herd in the States. An' I've got a market for 'em already.'

That was a long speech for Tom. Mack was duly impressed but didn't feel himself at all honoured. He couldn't think of anything to do except grunt in an interested way. And he was interested, mighty interested. With his words Big Tom had built up a picture in the young man's mind. A picture of a mean embittered old cripple man, an old cattle-baron squatting in his fortress like a sick spider, contemplating *his* wealth, *his* herds, *his* ruthless fighting men, and gloating over the power they all gave to him. He hadn't built up his empire by 'book-larnin',' but he wanted his daughter to be cleverer than any of them, to inherit his riches and power when he died and be Queen of them all. And here was Big Tom, who hated all old coyotes of ranchers with their milk-and-white daughters, and loved cattle and money too, bringing his Loboes along to smash that empire. Mack's lips quirked cynically. He was going to enjoy this job. He always wondered how and where Tom got all his information. But he had quit worrying about it. He was a gunfighter, not a detective.

With a raised arm that looked like the stout bough of a tree the Lobo leader halted his men.

'Listen,' he said.

They listened. 'Beef' said one …. 'Yeh – yeh' …. Everybody heard it now. Faintly with the wind came the mournful bellowing of cattle.

'It's a long way off yet,' Tom told them. 'It's a mighty big herd. It's a mighty big prize and it's well guarded by picked night-riders with itching trigger-fingers. Our only chance to pull off this job successfully an' without a lotta grief to ourselves, is to take 'em by surprise. I want yuh to spread out a bit now so's you won't jostle an' jingle. Travel at a walking pace an' no gabbin'. When we get near enough I'll give the word an' we'll split up intuh three sections. Got it, all of yuh?'

'All right. Spread out an' let's get moving.'

The Loboes were past-masters at the art of stealth, and their horses were well-trained too. They travelled for another half-mile or so with little more sound than the swishing of slow hooves through grass and the occasional creaking of leather.

In the distance a small red light swelled and winked and glittered. Big Tom held up his hand once more. The lowing of the big herd came very much clearer now, the sound booming and fluctuating with the wind.

'Mack,' said Big Tom. 'Cut yourself off a third of the bunch. Quickly. Over here with Mack some of yuh … Johnny Logan!'

'Yeh, boss.' Logan hove up out of the darkness.

'Cut yourself a bunch. I'll take the rest an' we'll make for the fire.'

As silently as possible the men sorted themselves out until Mack was at the head of one bunch, Johnny with the other. The rest clustered round the big Lobo.

'I want you two to take your men in opposite directions. Make a wide detour and flank the herd. It's your jobs to deal with the night riders. When you meet up, if you've done your jobs properly you'll know that all the night-riders have been dealt with. Try to avoid a lot of shooting, we don't want a stampede on our hands. When you've met make right away for the camp fire. I hope to meet you there. Yuh ready?'

'Yeh,' said Logan.

Mack echoed this laconic rejoinder.

'Get goin' then. I'll give you as much time as I think you need. None of us'll do any shootin' if we can help it.'

The two bunches led by the rival *segundas* set off, and the night swallowed them up.

'C'mon, boys,' said Big Tom. 'Gently does it.' Only he knew how really tough the job was going to be.

Old Idaho rode beside Mack Danvers. They travelled at a steady lope, making a wide half-circle, the others streaming along behind them. Presently Mack halted them with a raised hand. He rose in the stirrups. The bawling of cattle was much clearer now.

He looked over to the right of him, to where the campfire gleamed dully.

'I guess this is about it I reckon, Idaho,' he said.

'Yeh, I guess it is.'

Mack turned, speaking urgently. 'Split up, boys, intuh pairs. Fan out. Take it gently from here. You know what tuh do without a gink like me havin' tuh tell yuh.'

They did. Silently they went to it and pair by pair vanished like wraiths into the night. And Mack and Idaho were left alone.

'Let's get moving, old timer,' said the young man and kneed his horse gently forward.

They reached the herd, a dense, billowing mass in the darkness. There were no riders in sight.

The young man and the old eased their horses gently alongside the outer ring of steers. They bent low in the saddle, trying to hide themselves against the dark heaving mass. In this fashion they travelled slowly along. Idaho had gotten in front now but Mack kept close to his tail. This was the younker's first really big cattle raid, but the old Lobo had probably been on dozens of them. It was he who saw the night riders first and flapped a warning hand back at his companions. Then the younker spotted them. Two of them. He drew one of his guns. He noted that Idaho had drawn his too.

Then the moon, which had been hidden for the last

fifteen minutes or so, chose that moment to take a peek and flooded that part of the range with a sudden pale light. One of the nightriders spotted the two Loboes.

'Hey!' he said.

'All right, boys,' said Idaho gruffly. 'The boss sent us.'

But a gun already glinted in the man's hand. Idaho fired from the hip. It was the first – and fatal – shot of the night and it knocked its man from the saddle. Mack was already spurring his horse at a gallop. Even as the other man raised his gun Mack's horse caught his beast broadside. The shock was great. The man teetered in the saddle, his gun waving. The barrel of Mack's weapon caught him in the side of the head and finished the job.

But the damage had been done. The shot had been heard. Others followed it. The cattle began to bawl louder and shift restlessly.

'Come on, Idaho,' said Mack. They rode at a gallop, guns ready, eyes alert.

Mack had counted three more shots since Idaho's. Now he was riding at breakneck speed against the wind, which blustered and buffeted at him, making hearing difficult. He knew steers were bawling and stamping and horses hoofs were thudding, but it was all tied up with the chest-thumping brawling of the elements.

The moon came out again and the young man and the old seemed to be speeding along in a silver river. Then a horse and rider broke into the limelight before them. The rider's mouth was wide open and he was yelling but the wind whipped his words away. The moonlight gave the open-mouthed features a shimmering contorted aspect. Mack, not sure whether it was one of Johnny Logan's men held his horse in suddenly. Flame spurted past the other beast's neck and Mack felt the wind of the slug. He triggered savagely in return. The man's face crumpled, his eyes widened horribly. He fell from the saddle.

Idaho's crazed riderless horse crashed into Mack's beast. Turning Mack saw his old friend lying in the grass. The nearest cattle were bellowing frantically and beginning to move.

Mack did not have to dismount to find out about Idaho. The old man was lying on his back. The heavy slug had hit him in the middle of his face. And the moon was not merciful.

With a bitter curse Mack turned his horse again and rode on. Now the moving cattle almost kept pace with his horse. But the rider hardly noticed them.

Another horseman came in view, veering away from the herd, lying low over his horse's neck. Mack heard shots and saw another rider behind the first one. The second rider was Johnny Logan and he was doing the shooting.

Here was another night-rider trying to get away and give the alarm. Mack turned his horse's head and rode to intercept the man.

The fleeing man turned in the saddle and snapped a shot behind him. He missed. Mack held his fire. He wanted to be sure. One shot should do it.

The man turned again as his pursuer got closer. Mack felt the wind of the slug this time. He raised his gun. Then a giant fist seemed to smite him in the back, knocking him from his horse into space. As he hit the ground and rolled he felt hot, sickening pain. Far above him he saw the face of Johnny Logan, grinning in the moonlight. What a fool he'd been! What a fool to turn his back …

The moon had gone in. There was a rushing, roaring noise as of a huge herd of cattle in a mass stampede. Then no more sight or sound. Only utter blackness.

88

# CHAPTER SEVEN

The next sensation he felt was a swaying, jolting one, while sharp knives jabbed agonizingly, with sickening monotony into his back. There was that familiar pungent smell in his nostrils once more. He realised with remarkable clarity that he was slung across the back of a horse. He was getting used to being treated in this fashion. He was alive anyway, but in his agony he figured maybe it wouldn't be long before he was the other thing. Lady Luck was certainly turning her back on him lately. He was getting tired of being beaten down. Maybe he would be better dead.

As if in derision at his thoughts the pain and nausea was intensified. Overcome by it he lapsed once more into merciful unconsciousness.

There was flaming light around him when he came to again. He thought the fires of Hell were yawning to receive him. Then he realised the garish, flickering light came from torches, held in the hands of human men, not devils. But hard-faced men to boot, their mouths curling and opening, their cheeks pitted and shadowed by the flames, their eyes gleaming. They were all around him. Behind them he thought he saw the log walls of buildings.

Two cowhands lifted Mack from the horse and the mob

set up an argumentative clamouring which to the dazed wounded man sounded like the clattering and neighing of a herd of horses.

The two cowhands held him but others grabbed and clawed at him. The clamouring became louder. It seemed to Mack to be rising and falling in sickening spirals, all tied up with the pain and the terrible helplessness.

He was hoisted on to the horse once more, this time astride. A horseman came each side of him and held him on. The clamouring died to a fluctuating murmur. They moved forward.

They stopped again in the wide doorway of a feed-barn. When Mack raised his head everything he saw was blurred and swimming. But he could smell the hay, the old unforgettable odour that made him feel like bursting into tears. But he was too helpless even to do that.

Rough fingers fumbled at his collar. Then something buffeted his head, rasped on his face and neck. It was a rope, a noose around his neck. He heard the swish of it as its other end was tossed over a beam.

He raised his head and his vision cleared. He tried to fight but could not. He croaked, trying to tell them not to do it. He didn't want to die this way. But he saw their faces now, ruddy and awesome in the torchlight, and he knew they'd go through with it anyway.

Then they were shifting, looking behind them to where a shrill voice could be heard.

The hands that were holding Mack let go of him. He slumped forward across the horse's neck. The rope cut into his neck but he managed to turn his head.

His interest made him forget his agony and peril as he heard the sharp voice cry: 'Let me thru'.'

The torches wavered, the ranks broke, and a tawny-haired woman broke into the circle of light. She had a quirt in her hand and she swung it as she shouted: 'The man's badly wounded. Let him down, you cowards!'

A big florid-faced man started forward.

'Now, Miss Judy, this ain't none o' your business. This is man's business. This hombre's a killer an' he's got to be finished.'

'Let the law see to that,' snapped the girl. 'You're not going to lynch a sick man. Let him down I say.'

The big man moved closer and caught hold of the girl's arm. 'Now come on, Miss Judy.'

'How dare you, Hapwood,' shrilled the girl. 'Take your paws off me.'

She tore herself away from him. The quirt in her hand rose and fell. The man started back, clutching his cheek.

'Let him down,' screamed the girl.

The torches moved nearer. Hands pulled at Mack. They were far from gentle. He passed out again.

He had run the old gamut of fantastic sensations. This new one was not ideal – the pain was still there – but at least it was an improvement on previous ones. The blankets under which he lay were soft, warm and soothing. They were also spotlessly clean. He was lying on his back, but by turning his head could see around him. His vision swam, then cleared slowly.

He was in a bedroom: he had never seen a bedroom quite like it before. It wasn't that it was luxurious, it wasn't even brightly coloured and showy like some of the rooms he had seen in big saloons and other places. The all-over effect was one of startling cleanliness and light. At first the right word with which to describe it eluded Mack. Then he plumped on the one. It was not a word he was accustomed

91

to and tripped clumsily off his tongue. It was '*refinement*'.

He heard the door of the room open and tried to jerk his head to see it. He winced and had a sudden attack of giddiness.

'Feeling kind of sick, young man?' said a gruff voice.

A big red face with a ring of snowy-white hair hovered above him. It surmounted a broad swelling torso in spotless white linen and black broadcloth with a neatly tied shoestring cravat. Shrewd blue eyes looked down at him with interest that was merely professional.

'A doc,' said Mack hoarsely.

'Yeh, a doc,' said the man. ' I asked you if you felt kind of sick.'

'Yeh, kinda. How much chance have I got, doc?'

'You got a good chance o' getting better from the wound in your back,' said the doctor noncommittally.

'Have you got a cigarette?' said Mack.

'Cigar?'

'Sure, thanks.'

The doctor took one from his top-pocket, snapped the end off with a natty little pair of shears, popped it in Mack's mouth and lit it for him.

The young man puffed gratefully. 'That's good,' he said.

'It's a good cigar,' said the doctor. Then: 'Are you comfortable?'

'Yeh, thanks.' The doctor really sounded as if he wanted to know.

'Feel like a bite and something to drink?'

'Yeh, sure.'

'All right,' said the doctor. 'I'll come in and see you again later on.'

The door banged again. Mack puffed at the cigar. Fancy

a doctor like that one being interested in him. He was a killer, they wanted to hang him. He felt cynical again. He tried to grin and couldn't quite make it. The doc was just fattening him up for the slaughter because that woman had had scruples about stringing-up a wounded man. Still, he had to hand it to her; she had saved his life, given him a chance to enjoy this cigar and the meal that was to follow it. Why fret about what was to come after? His pain was not severe now just a nagging throb which he wouldn't let bother him a lot. It was kind of peaceful here. He'd make the most of it – while he'd got it.

He finished the cigar. He turned his head. There was even an ashtray on the small table at his side. He ground the stub in this small copper bowl with the queer signs around its rim.

The door opened again. Feet tapped on the floor. A pair of smooth brown arms, small slim-fingered hands, put a tray of eatables and steaming coffee on the bedside table. The girl stood before him. Her face was set and she did not look at him. So he had plenty of chance to look her over.

She was slim in her white shirtwaist and dark grey skirt. She looked wiry but she had all the curves too. Her face was brown, boyish, with high cheekbones and large dark eyes. She was almost Indian-looking. Some Indian girls are very beautiful. But they got fat and ugly as they got older. Mack knew this girl would never be that way. Her hair was long and tawny with little glints in it. It was well-groomed in a smooth sweeping way but there was nothing artificial about it.

This was Judy, old crippled Kit Maxton's 'milk-and-white' daughter. This was the girl who had saved his life. She wasn't what he had expected. Last night – he supposed it had been last night – he had got only a confused impression of a screeching woman, a spitfire. Now she looked just a kid who was trying to be severe and competent.

Mack had a sudden impulse. He said: 'I want tuh thank you for what you did for me, ma'am. I guess you saved my bacon.'

'Please forget it,' she said.

Her voice was very different too. It was a husky murmur with a subtle something in it, a quality that evaded Mack's full comprhenesion. He figured it must come from being educated.

She spoke again. 'The doctor says you mustn't try to sit up yet. If I prop your head up with more pillows and place the tray on your chest do you think you can manage?'

'I guess so.'

She left him returning almost immediately with two more pillows. Mack raised his head and she propped them beneath him. She placed the tray on the bed well within his reach. She was very smart about it.

'Fine,' he said. 'Thanks.'

'I'd do the same for a crippled dog,' she said.

It was a sudden cruel thrust. She left the room quickly as if she was ashamed she had said it.

For a moment Mack felt as if he had been kicked in the guts. Then he shrugged and attacked the contents of the tray. But his mind would not let him forget it. It made him feel like a whipped no-account cur must feel. Why the hell did he have a mind like that?

When the girl came to collect the tray she did not speak to him. Nor him to her. They avoided each other's eyes. When she had gone he moved the two extra pillows from beneath his head himself and lay staring at the ceiling. He wanted to get out of this bed, right out of this room and back to the Ant Heap and the Loboes, the people he understood. But he could only move his head and his arms. To move any other part of his body caused him agony. He guessed he'd never see the Lobo camp again. He guessed that within a few weeks from now he'd either be swinging on the end of a rope or caged-up in a prison cell. That is if he didn't died in the meantime. Maybe it would be better that way.

He wondered idly how the Loboes had fared on the raid. It was with little interest. His only regret was that now he'd never be able to kill Johnny Logan. The black-faced coyote had certainly come out top-dog after all.

Mack saw a lot of the girl. She spoke to him only when necessary and then in monosyllables. But she looked after him well. He learnt from the doctor, whose name was Greaves, that she had taken a course in nursing while she was back East. She was certainly getting in plenty of practise right now. Mack began to mend at what the doc said was an astonishing rate. His strong constitution and mercurial temperament would not let him stay under for long.

On his third or maybe it was his fourth day, he was visited by Kit Maxton, the owner of Loop W. The old man looked everything he was reckoned to be. He was pushed into the room in a wheelchair by a poker-faced two-gun man who didn't make a single sound during the whole of the interview.

Old Maxton was little and withered and  hunched. He looked like a little old monkey, wrapped in a voluminous shawl, crouched up in the chair which was a lot too big for him. His face was yellow and hairless and dried up. The mean, pinched up look on it gave the impression all the workings inside him were dried up too. His head was bald, except for a few stray strands like colourless weeds around his ears. Even his skull was yellowy-brown and wrinkled like a walnut shell. He had one fang and this showed viciously when he opened his lips to speak. The only things about him that seemed really, humanly alive were his eyes. They were small and squeezed up but they snapped wickedly when he was angry, they were the signs to go by and when they flashed his toughest rough-riders feared him and, in his malice, what he could do to them. For he was Czar of this territory; if he kicked them out they couldn't get another job for a hundred miles or so – or maybe much further if he willed it so, for he was untiring in his malice.

He said but a few words to the young man in the bed, words spoken brutally in an idiom the outlaw could well understand.

'My daughter snatched the rope from around your neck, young feller,' he said, his voice brittle but clear. 'She wouldn't've gotten out if I coulda stopped her. I'd've let you swing and stink like the young kyote you are. But she saved yuh and she insists on nursin' yuh till you're well. Maybe she jest wants somethin' to do. After that the law takes over. And, hear me, I'll make it my personal task to see that you walk to the gallows.'

'Thanks, pop,' said Mack. 'It'll be a pleasure tuh walk anyway.'

But the old man had said his piece and he was unmoved by such facetiousness. The eyes had gone dull, his lids drooped, he might have been dead. The poker-face gunny turned the chair and wheeled him from the room.

Their place was taken, almost immediately, by a big

man with a protruding undercarriage, a heavy low-slung gun that made him look lopsided and a beautiful black walrus moustache. He had a big tin star right prominent on the right-hand breast of his fancy vest.

He introduced himself as Clem Poynton, sheriff of this county. He wanted some information. He promised the young feller that he personally would see things went a bit easier for him if he told the law where to find the rustling band. Mack said that this morning he was plumb tired of listening to promises. The sheriff could, very impolitely, go to hell.

The sheriff retaliated, very spitefully, by assuring the young feller that his pards hadn't gotten away with anything anyway. The cattle had stampeded. The Loop W boys had probably rounded 'em all up by now. One of the rustlers had been trampled to death in the stampede, another one, an old man, had been found with his face shot away.

Three night-riders had been shot. Mack would take the rap for that unless he passed it on to somebody else. Who was his boss? Where did he come from? Where was the gang's hideout?

'You make me tired,' said Mack. He closed his eyes. 'Go an' jump in a crick,' he added laconically.

The sheriff rose in his wrath and towered over the bed.

'You young pup,' he said. 'I'll see you swing.'

He stamped from the room.

Mack continued to lie with his eyes closed. The stinging phrase the girl had used that first day flashed through his mind. Yeh, everybody treated him like a dog. A mad dog. Yes, even the girl herself. She handled him as if he might bite her, as if he were a sick animal instead of a human being. Her and her fancy Eastern nursing. Fattening up the beast for slaughter.

Doc Greaves was the only one who, the last couple of times he saw him anyway, treated him like something human. The old Doc had probably met up with all kinds in his time. He acted like a gent – but he didn't always talk like one. Mack had begun to sense in him something of a kindred spirit. Thinking of it again now it seemed a plumb foolish idea ....

Presently Greaves himself entered. 'How are you feeling now, son?' he said.

'Fine, doc.'

The white-haired doctor crossed to the bedside and put a plump strong arm beneath Mack's head. 'Try and sit up,' he said.

Mack tried, grimacing with pain. But with the help of the other man he managed it.

'Rest easy,' said the old man. He fetched two pillows and put them behind the patient's shoulders.

'That all right?'

'Sure, doc. Thanks.'

Greaves drew a chair up beside the bed and sat down. He produced a couple of the inevitable cigars. He handed one over. They lit up.

They puffed for a time in silence. Then the doc said: 'You should be able to get out o' bed in another few days. But you won't be able to walk around much .... Maybe old Kit will lend you one of his wheelchairs.' Mack had learnt the doctor was fond of making cryptic remarks such as that last one.

Mack did not speak. The old jackass seemed inclined to talk. He waited for the next sample. It was typical of the old man's directness.

'How old are you, son?'

'Twenty, I guess.'

'Kind of young to be riding the owlhoot trail aren't you? You don't *look* like a skunk.'

'Quit flattering me,' said Mack. For the first time in many days he grinned. 'If I'd got a gun I'd probably blow your head off.'

Doc ignored this. 'I met Billy the Kid once,' he said conversationally. 'He wuz younger than you. But he looked every bit of what he was. He wasn't human. He was a robot with two arms that worked like pistons, drawing and shooting, that's all he knew. He was a gun fighting beast, a gun wolf.'

Those last words sent a sudden shock through Mack. Was that what he had gotten to be? – a gun wolf! Billy the Kid had been a lone wolf. But wolves usually hunted in packs. Like the Loboes. Their name, the name they had chosen for themselves, fitted them well.

The doc was talking again. 'How did you come to be an owlhooter, son?'

'Jest by accident I guess,' said Mack, haltingly.

The old man inclined his head and looked interested. Suddenly Mack found himself telling him the whole story. He hadn't meant to. It just came out. Maybe it was because Doc Greaves was the only one who treated him right. The only one who was interested in him. Maybe it was because he had never talked to anyone like this before, never told anyone all of it before. Maybe it was just that he felt like talking and the story of his life, short though it was, didn't need no thinking out, no fancy talking-frills.

Maybe it had to be told to somebody before he cashed in his chips. Although he wouldn't admit it to himself maybe he kind of pitied himself a little. He'd never had much of a chance. He evaded the fact now that most of the time he had enjoyed the thrill and excitement of living by the gun, had preened himself with pride in his own speed on the draw, the chance to kill or be killed, knowing that the odds were mostly against the other man. He had been confident and alive. And he had been pretty happy except for now and again towards the last.

He told the doc about Jed Benson, his uncle whom he hated. Others hated him too and one night one of those enemies got him. Kid though he was Mack had been out riding on the line that night. It was from friendly neighbours that he heard of his uncle's murder and that the law was after *him* for it. He got scared and bolted. He got away and rode in a panic for a day and a night. Then during a howling storm he stumbled into the outlaw camp. At this part of his narrative he gave no names and used no descriptions. He halted. His story hadn't been long. He was already getting near to its end.

The doc said: 'Didn't you have any other folks except this uncle of yours?'

'Nope. I never knew any folks but him. My maw and paw were killed in a fire when I wuz a baby. Uncle Jed brought me up on his farm. He made me earn everything I had from him. An' I paid interest in kicks and lashings. He seemed tuh like to beat me up. He was made that way I guess. He seemed tuh like people to hate him and he didn't want me tuh be left out of the runnin'.'

'I've met men like that,' said the doc half to himself.

'I did hate him,' said Mack. 'But I didn't kill him .... I guess I never felt that way in them days,' he added sardonically.

'How many men have you killed since, son?' said the doc.

The question was unexpected. Mack did not answer it right off.

Finally he said: 'Four I guess,' softly. Then his voice rose. 'But they all had an even break, doc. I'll swear that.'

'You're fast, I guess.'

'Yeh, I'm fast,' Mack told him. Then vanity spoke before he could stop it. 'I beat John M. Madin tuh the draw.'

'Madin!' Doc Greaves looked surprised. 'I heard about that. A ranger was killed and a stranger.'

Inwardly Mack cursed himself. 'I didn't do none o' that. They shot each other tuh death. The stranger was a pard of mine. I guess he saved my life.' He pulled up short then. He was telling too much. He flapped his mouth and words streamed out. He was like Billy the Kid, all he could do properly was tote a gun.

'Somebody is always saving your life,' said Doc Greaves dryly.

They talked together a while more and said nothing. Then the doc got up and left.

It was nearing sundown when Mack had his next visitor. It was another new one, a big florid-faced man, who came in with his hat in his hand. His face looked vaguely familiar but Mack could swear that he had never been in this room before. He introduced himself as Matt Hapwood. He was the straw boss around here.

Then Mack remembered. This was the man the girl had quirted, the man who wanted to hang him. What did he want? Was this the beginning of another attempt?

But no, Hapwood wanted to hear his life story as well. He was mighty polite about it too, he was glad the feller was feeling well enough to chat. Maybe he (Hapwood) had been a mite hasty that night. Some of his men had been killed, the cattle were a-running .... Still, every man

101

ought to have a chance of a fair trial, he realised that now.

He was a real friendly cuss. Nevertheless, as Mack parried question after question his tone became more hectoring. So Mack shut up.

Then Hapwood changed his tune once more, became obliquely conversational. He couldn't understand a young feller like Mack being on the owlhoot. There was always a place for a young gunny, especially on a big ranch, the Loop W for instance, as long as he played it straight. Toting a gun for a big legitimate outfit was better than being on the run .... There might be a chance even now. He had plenty of pull with the old man. And the old man was the law around here in spite of anything that fat stupid sheriff said. If Mack sort of played along, maybe Hapwood .... Anyway, any little thing he could do would help to make up for that night.

'Wal, pardner, if there's anything you can do I'd be mighty grateful for it,' said Mack blandly.

Hapwood eyed him suspiciously. At this juncture the door opened and Judy Maxton entered. Hapwood started to his feet.

'What are you doing here?' she said. 'Planning another lynching? Investigating to see if the prospective victim is fit enough?'

'Aw, Miss Judy,' spluttered the straw boss. 'I sort of came to apologise.'

A faint smile crossed the girl's face. It disconcerted Hapwood. He shuffled past her and out through the door.

'Somebody loves me anyway,' said Mack.

'Just what did you mean by that remark?' she said.

He shrugged. 'Just a passing thought,' he said. He was gratified that she had deigned to speak to him in a lighter manner. It made him feel less of a no-account in her presence. Though why he should bother at all about things like that, he couldn't figure. He shouldn't bother about what she thought of him …. Why then *did* he get that no-account feeling when she was around and was so glad of a few carelessly tossed words.

She said: 'What *did* he want?'

'Like he said,' responded Mack, 'he sort of came to apologise.'

She was openly scornful. 'And what else?'

'He asked me a lot of fool questions and I gave him a lot of fool answers.'

'You're smart aren't you,' she snapped. 'What kind of questions?'

'The same kind of questions the law asked. Only Hapwood asked them in a different way.'

'Oh,' said the girl. She did not speak again but as she did little things for him she seemed preoccupied.

# CHAPTER EIGHT

Two days later Mack got out of bed. In that time he did not see Hapwood or the sheriff again. Doc Greaves came a few times and the girl was in and out constantly. Her preoccupied manner was still with her; perhaps it was just a pose, a shield against him. However, when she spoke to him now her husky voice was a little less indifferent, a little more human. He tried to get her into more intimate conversation but she shied away from that like a scared colt. Mack felt frustrated and cursed himself for being so.

The first day he sat in a chair beside the bed. He sat there till sundown then crawled stiffly between the sheets. His muscles were flabby and aching, his body was like a tired old man's. But with much sweating and cursing he made it by himself that time.

The doc had supplied him with voluminous pyjamas, also a razor and a comb. Why the old man took such trouble with a young owlhoot Mack could not figure. He got some inkling of the answer to this question when Greaves, who had come to sit with him for a while said:

'Mack, do you know Big Tom Heineman?'

The question was even more unexpected than others the doc had shot at him from time to time. Mack could not disguise the terrific shock of surprise it gave him. He did not answer right off.

'You do know him don't you, son?' said Greaves.

'Yeh, I know him. Why, what's happened to him?'

'Nothing as far as I know. But Sheriff Clem Poynton has got a reward notice for him. He's wanted for everything in the book.'

'Yeh?' said Mack.

'Bank robbery, train robbery, rustling, murder. He's reckoned to be running the biggest and most perfectly trained band of outlaws in the State. Everybody's pretty certain it was his gang that raided the Loop W. Now *I know* it was.'

'I ought to've kept my trap shut,' snarled Mack. 'But it's no good you askin' me where they're hiding out 'cos I shan't tell yuh.'

'I know that, son,' said Greaves softly. 'I never meant to ask. The whole brood ought to be stamped out. But that's the sheriff's job not mine. I guess I'm a soft-hearted sentimental old man and wouldn't like to have a hand in it. You see, I know Big Tom Heineman as well. Or at least I used to.'

Mack's eyes showed interest. He leaned forward. 'I'd like to hear about that, doc.'

Greaves handed him a cigar and took one himself. He produced his little clippers and they nipped off the ends of the weeds. They lit up.

The doc puffed for a while then he said:

'Big Tom and I were young men together. He was younger than I. Where we lived doesn't really matter. It was cow-country. Big Tom was made for the cow-country. He wanted to be a top-line stockman and studied for it. Young as he was he got to be one of the best buyers in the territory. He used to read a lot too, swot at nights, got himself educated. I wanted to be a doctor and I went away to study. While I was away Tom got married. That was his first mistake. She was no good but Tom didn't find out till later....'

'Not till she ran off with another man,' put in Mack.

'You know about that?'

'Yeh. An' I know about how he went after them and killed them both.'

'Yes, he must have gone berserk. When the law tried to take him he shot an officer. After that he dropped out of sight for about a year. Lots of his friends thought he must be dead. Really it's only just lately that we have become sure he's still alive – and we know what he's doing.' Doc Greaves shook his head slowly, sadly.

Mack's brain was working furiously, things were fitting together. He said sharply 'Doc, did you know Jeb McCloud, the banker of Garret's Gulch.'

Greaves did not seem surprised at the question. 'Yes I knew Jeb. He was about the same age as myself, a pard of Tom's too, he even saved Tom's life once. That's why I was shocked when I heard of the Garret's Gulch robbery and Jeb's murder. By the description circulated of the leader of the bandits I knew it could not be anybody else but Heineman. And he killed his old friend, the man to whom he owed his life.'

'He didn't kill him, he tried to prevent it,' said Mack. 'And afterwards he slaughtered the man who'd done it.'

Mack remembered suddenly with painful clarity Big Tom's contorted face as in a berserk rage he shot down Pinto Cabot.

'Despite everything he led the raid,' said the doctor. 'Even if his wasn't the hand that fired the gun he was directly responsible for old Jeb's death.'

'He didn't know it was Jeb McCloud's bank until we got inside. I remember how surprised he was when the old man confronted him,' said Mack. 'Still,' he sighed, 'I guess you're right. He was to blame …. But, if it's any consolation tuh you, Doc, he was mighty sorry afterwards. He wasn't the same man afterwards, I guess it worried him a whole lot.'

'Because I'm a soft-hearted old cuss and don't easily forget old friends I guess I'd like to think it worried him a whole lot,' said the doc.

'I've got no cause to lie to you,' said Mack.

'No, I guess you haven't.' The old man rose heavily. He stubbed the remains of his cold cigar in the ashtray. 'I'll be seeing you later, son,' he said as he left the room.

The girl entered with a meal on a tray. She said: 'I shan't be coming to see you much longer. Father's creating about it again. He says you don't need nursing.'

'Maybe I don't,' said Mack. 'But it sure was pleasurable bein' nursed. I want to thank you again for all you've done.'

She did not answer him but turned away and began to lay the meal on the small table.

Looking up Mack could see her smooth brown cheek and the firm line of her chin. The way her long tawny hair curled around her ear and swept back and down almost to her shoulders. The firm column of her neck, soft and brown in the open-necked shirtwaist. Her firm breasts as she turned, her straight shoulders and slim waist. All these things were very appealing to him. Despite her Eastern education she was first rate Frontier stock. She hadn't *had* to do all this for him. Mack wanted to tell her again, to make her understand how grateful he was for the time he had had here, irrespective of what came after. But he felt suddenly choked up and inarticulate .... Not another word had passed between them when the door closed behind her.

Mack sat immobile looking at it. Then finally he shrugged. A real tough two-gun hombre he was – letting a gel haze him thataway. He turned to his meal. Gosh, he felt durned hungry.

When he had finished he had another smoke, rolling one of his own quirlies this time. Then he rose, he could do that quite easily now, and limped slowly round the room. Yesterday he had gone round the bed three times. This time he made it five. Then he crossed to the window.

His room was on the second storey. It looked out across the yard to the corral. A few hands were getting on with their jobs down there. Familiar sounds came up through the open window.

The log walls of the ranch house were rough. There were plenty of foot and hand-holds. If he was fit enough it would be easy for him to climb to the ground. He wondered what would happen if he was seen doing that. Those hands would collar him in no time or shoot him as he made a run for it. He was a prisoner all right; just a useless hulk waiting for the rope. He felt suddenly tired and went back to his chair.

At nights his thoughts were always more bitter. The nights were silent and still, and the scent of the range seemed stronger, the sage, the pungent smell of animals, a whiff of wood-smoke. It all came through the open window with the cool breeze; and the moonlight dappling the walls was all part of it too. Western nights at this time of the year were pretty grand. It was only when a fellow was cooped up

108

in a room like this that he really began to appreciate them. However, there was something lacking in this particular one ....

The breeze was the same, the smell was the same, but there was no moonlight. Mack missed the silver flood, the shimmering pathway the changing patterns on the wall. And he couldn't sleep.

It was late when he heard the sound at the window and turned to look that way. He saw the faint outline of a big head surmounted by a Stetson. Then a wide pair of shoulders came through the window, and a pair of arms. Something glinted in the man's hand. Mack hadn't got a gun and he felt helpless and almost panicky. But he lay still, hardly daring to breathe, just staring.

There was something very familiar about that form. Only one man could have a body and head as big as that.

Then the voice spoke softly. 'Mack.'

'Tom,' he breathed. 'Here.'

The rest of Big Tom's massive length came through the window turned slowly and came towards him. Mack got out of bed.

'Get dressed, Mack,' said the Lobo leader. 'We've got no time to lose.'

'They've taken my clothes away,' whispered the younker. 'I've only got pyjamas and a dressing-gown.'

'I kinda figured on that,' said Tom. He went back to the window and hissed. He leaned out. Then he returned with a bundle which he passed to Mack. There was everything the young man needed.

'I've got guns and a belt for you down below,' said Tom. 'Hurry it up. Here, I'll help you.'

'You'll have to,' Mack told him. 'I'm kinda weak. I guess you'll have to drop me outa that window.'

'We can fix that with a rope.'

Barely five minutes later Mack was being helped along by Big Tom and four more Loboes. They half-carried him, half-walked him to where they had left the horses at the back of the corral. Once in the saddle with the night wind blowing in his face Mack felt a whole lot better. The reins gripp    his hands gave him new strength, the smooth bel    he horse between his legs. And the guns  at his hi    ve him confidence.

They made a wide detour to avoid the herd and the night-riders. They had a long way to travel and, well before dawn, put up at a small hotel on the outskirts of a town.

The following morning they started off again. They spotted the Ant Heap sticking up out of the foothills like some abnormal growth long before they reached it. The sight of it gave new heart to the weary, aching young Lobo who was returning to it.

They reached the camp at noon. Just in time for the midday meal. But Mack was not hungry. All he wanted to do now was rest up, and as soon as the greetings and congratulations were all finished with, he flopped down on his bunk. Right now it seemed infinitely more comfortable than any feather bed. He sank like a stone into deep, dreamless slumber.

When he awoke it was as if he had never left the crude log cabin in the valley with its rows of bunks, its rickety deal table, its broken chairs, its rough board floor. It was like that time after his fight with Johnny Logan. It was funny he had stopped thinking about Johnny a few days ago. Naturally, Johnny hadn't been among the mob who welcomed him home.

Mack had not told anyone yet who it was who had shot him in the back. He wondered what Johnny was doing, somewhere in the camp, right now. Getting ready to have another try maybe …. When the men learnt about his treachery what would be their reactions? Maybe it would be better if Johnny started to ride while the going was good. Either that or prevent the story from ever being told.

With thoughts like that in his mind it was little wonder that Mack reached for his gun as the bunkhouse door opened But it was only Big Tom.

'Tom,' said Mack instantly. 'Where's Johnny Logan?'

'He got killed in that cattle stampede during the raid,' said the big man. 'Didn't you know?'

'I knew somebody got trampled to death,' Mack said. 'But I didn't know it was Logan.'

So he didn't have to kill Johnny after all. Johnny was dead. Suddenly Mack felt relieved. Killing Johnny hadn't been so very important after all. It was better this way.

He told Tom of Logan's treachery. The Lobo leader was surprised. He and all his men had thought Mack got shot by one of the Loop W night-riders. It was only by scouting around, afterwards, that they discovered Mack had survived and was a prisoner in the ranch house.

'Hardly a prisoner,' said the young man. 'I was treated mighty nicely considering what I was. The old man's daughter nursed me like a baby. When I get well enough I want to go back there and thank her. I don't want her to think I run out on her.'

'Run out on her,' echoed Big Tom blankly. 'Are you going plumb loco? Have your experiences turned your brain or somethin'. I always told you never to trust a woman?'

But Mack was stubborn. 'She could've let me be hanged in the first place,' he said. He told of how she had saved him from the lynch-mob.

'Squeamishness,' snorted Tom. 'Maybe she was lonely and wanted somethin' to do. Nursing you was it.'

Mack knew it was no use arguing with Big Tom on the subject of women. He changed the subject, saying suddenly: 'Doc Greaves was mighty nice to me too,.'

'Doc Greaves,' echoed the big man. Mack could see by his face that the name had struck a chord in his mind. He took a chance.

'Yeh, Doc Greaves,' he repeated. 'Him who used to be your pardner.'

Tom sat down suddenly. 'Him. He told you about it?'

'Most of it,' said Mack. 'An' about Jeb McCloud. Now I know why you killed Pinto Cabot. I guess maybe I'd've done the same myself.'

'Would you?' said the Lobo leader dully. 'I guess you would. But killing Pinto didn't bring ol' Jeb back. I was to blame all along for his death. That's why I shot Pinto I guess. But it wasn't Pinto's fault. It was mine. Jeb saved my life once.'

'Yeh, I know. Doc Greaves told me.'

'You know it all don't you?' said the big man. He paused then: – 'An' you know why I took to the owlhoot trail. But it's no good. For a man of intelligence it's no good. Get out of it quick before you get in as deep as I am.'

'I never expected to hear that from you, Tom.'

'Well, you're hearing it all right,' said Tom harshly. 'I don't want to lose you, Mack, but why worry about me. I got six months, a year, maybe two years to live. Somebody'll get me sooner or later. But you've got your life before you – if you play it right an' don't make a fool of yourself like I did. Get out I say!'

The big man rose and hurried away. The door slammed behind him.

112

Mack remembered another older man who had told him the same things not so very long ago. An outlaw like Tom. Old Idaho, whose body lay now in an unmarked grave miles away. In his heart now Mack knew that Idaho had been right. Big Tom was right. Doc Greaves was right. Get out! But how? Wasn't he too far in? Wasn't he a member of the Loboes? – a wanted man!

Time, not Big Tom Heineman, did not shake Mack's resolve to return to the Loop W and say goodbye to the girl. He let his moustache grow again. The only thing that might give him away was his limp, a first legacy of his owl-hoot days that would stay with him for ever. Big Tom was sure the girl would give him away. But Mack was not scared of that. Anyway, he wouldn't be fool enough to approach her while she was in company. He knew from Doc Greaves that she went out riding alone very day. It was on one of those rides that he hoped to catch her.

Three weeks after his return to camp he was ready to ride right back to the Loop W again.

Big Tom was resigned. 'Well if you've made your mind up I guess you gotta go,' he said. 'Good luck to you, an' if you meet Doc Greaves give him my compliments. He at least won't turn you in.'

'No I guess not,' said Mack. 'So long, Tom. I'll be back.'

The Lobo leader watched him ride away. 'All fire an' guts,' he said softly to himself. 'I guess he will come back at that.'

It was night when Mack reached Benton City, the town on the outskirts of the Loop W land. Old Kit Maxton owned most of this town. Despite its grand title it wasn't a big place. But it did look prosperous and had a bigger share of new red-brick buildings than the average cow town.

Nevertheless, like all such places, it had its low dives. Mack found one of these, a flophouse in a dark cul-de-sac on the edge of town. He paid in advance for a room for a night. The fat, dirty-faced proprietor hardly looked at him but pocketed the money and handed over a key.

'Number Three,' he said.

No. 3 turned out to be fat and dirty like its keeper. Fat inasmuch that the faded wallpaper bulged alarmingly, dirty because it obviously hadn't been swept or dusted for weeks. There was a rim of dirt round the cracked basin on the washstand; the only other article of furniture besides the rusty iron bedstead, was a lopsided basket-chair. Mack was pleased to discover that despite its surroundings the bed linen though threadbare and of a greyish colour, was remarkably clean. It had evidently been changed recently.

He felt tired. He had been so eager to come on this trip, Big Tom's sneers only serving to drive him on – perhaps he had come a mite too soon. Still – no good going back now. Here he was within a few miles of the ranch-house that housed Judy Maxton .... He'd see how he felt in the morning. He only took off his boots, his hat, his gunbelt and his short jacket then he climbed between the sheets. He slept with a gun under his pillow.

The range shimmered in the afternoon sunshine, mile after unbroken mile of it, billowing and swelling to the blue haze of the horizon. This was the gentler part of Texas, where the sun was not too hot, the breeze blew but the storms did not rage. Cattle grew sleek and fat on the lush juicy grass and the bank-balance of their owner grew accordingly. Men said Kit Maxton was a millionaire.

He did not need to fence his land because he owned everything around. All the territory was his – much further

than the human eye could see. There were no wire fences,
no trespassing signs, but a stranger riding through was
always liable to be pounced on by Loop W gunhawks and
catechised till he gave adequate explanation of his business there. Mack Danvers did not have to be told this. He
knew Kit Maxton's sort too well, and he hated them as
much as Big Tom Heineman did. How a measly old coyote
like that horrible cripple up at the ranch-house ever came
to have a nice kid like Judy he could not rightly figure. Her
mother must have been a wonderful woman to stick a man
like that and produce a daughter like Judy to boot.

Mack Danvers rode warily across Loop W territory, his
yellow moustache blowing slightly in the breeze, and
looked for that daughter. Then he saw riders and had to
shy off. He did not see Judy that day.

That night he paid again for the use of No. 3.

'Just one night?' said the fat man.

'Yes, I guess so.'

'I can let you have the room cheaper if you book for a
week.'

'No, I don't expect I'll be stayin' that long.'

'How long you aiming to stay?'

'Not much longer I hope. I got to see a friend in town.
He hasn't turned up yet.'

'Oh.'

As Mack climbed the stairs he could feel the big man's
eyes on him. His back prickled, it was mighty sensitive.
Mack began to sweat. He turned his head.

'Goodnight,' said the fat man.

'Good-night.'

The next day he rode out on to Loop W range again.
This time, after half-an-hour of fruitless looking into the
sun, his sight was rewarded.

She was quite close to him before he saw her. She came riding straight for him, probably thinking he was one of the Loop W men. Then as she came closer her piquant, boyish face got a puzzled look.

Mack raised his hat. 'Afternoon, Miss Judy,' he said.

'Good afternoon,' she replied. Her voice was puzzled. She came closer. Mack realised it was the moustache that puzzled her. 'Are you a new man?' she said.

'Not exactly, ma'am.'

They were near to each other now. Suddenly her eyes widened, she gasped, she looked around her. There was nothing else but the limitless range.

'You don't have to be sacred o' me, Miss Judy,' said Mack. He felt a queer stab, almost physical pain at the thought that she feared him.

'What do you want?' she said. 'What have you come back for? They'll kill you if they catch you.'

'I came back to see you,' he said quickly. 'To thank you again for all you've done and to say good-bye. I didn't want you to think I'd gone to a thought. Sneaked away in the night. The boys came for me. They risked their lives tuh fetch me so I went with them. Could you blame me when I knew what to expect if I stayed here?'

Her eyes were frank. 'No I can't blame you,' she said. 'But the doctor was fighting for you. He meant you to get off lightly. He couldn't understand you going back to that life. Neither can I.'

'Did the doctor tell you my story.'

'Yes, he did.'

'That's the only life I've ever known. Couldn't you understand?'

'You're young,' she said simply. And he knew she was right. He had to bluster so he said:

116

'Your father's more powerful than the doctor and you know what he wanted to do with me don't you?'

Her face paled but she continued to look at him steadily. 'Yes I know,' she said. 'And I know what his men will do if they catch you. You'd better go now.'

'I'll go,' said Mack. He urged his horse nearer. 'If you ever need a friend....' It was foolish: This girl of power and riches would never need a friend like him. But he plunged on. '...You get in touch with me.' He stopped. But where? She was looking at him levelly, unsmiling, unspeaking.

'I saw a tree just outside Benton City,' he said quickly. 'An old one, the only tree for miles around. On the third of every month about this time in the afternoon I'll be there.'

He thrust out his hand and gripped hers. Then he turned his horse and galloped furiously off. Once back in Benton City he went into the flophouse and right back up to his room. Doc Greaves was sitting on the bed.

'Hallo, Mack,' he said. 'I came to give you the tip that Sheriff Poynton is coming to investigate Pecos's new boarder. I guessed it was you.'

'Thanks, doc. I was goin' anyway. Thanks for everythin'.' Mack paused then gave the old man Big Tom's message. The old man heard him in silence then got up to go.

'You seen Miss Judy?' he said.

'Yeh. This afternoon.'

'I guessed as much.' The doc shook his white head. from side to side slowly. Then he held out his hand.

'Good luck, Mack. And tell Tom good luck too – tho' I guess he doesn't deserve it.' The old man left.

When Sheriff Poynton and his two deputies came to the flophouse Pecos shrugged his fat shoulders. The stranger had gone.

# CHAPTER NINE

Mack gave Big Tom the message he had from old Doc Greaves. The Lobo leader was more delighted than his young pardner had ever seen him before.

'How is the ol' buzzard?' he said.

'He looked fine.'

'I'll have to go an' see for myself.'

'I shouldn't if I were you,' said Mack. 'They've got your description circulated in that territory. Five hundred dollars reward.'

'That all?' snorted Tom. ''The pikers.'

He was in a good humour but he sobered up when Mack told him of his meeting with the girl and his resolve to see her again.

'You're crazy,' said Tom. 'Either that or lovesick.'

'Whatdyuh mean?' Mack was annoyed.

'Just that. You're in love with the gel. It's the old, old story of the patient falling for his nurse.'

'Now *you're* crazy,' snarled Mack and turned away.

Big Tom began to guffaw. The younker felt like turning back and smacking him one, but he bottled up his rage and stamped on.

The big man's malicious thrust had got right under his

skin. But the galling thing about it all was that Big Tom might be right. Why else would he be so keen on seeing the girl again, risking his life to do so. Gratitude? She had made it quite plain that she did not need his gratitude. Help? What help could that heiress of power and wealth ever need from him?

For a short time his resolve weakened. But, as the week passed on it became stronger again, the jeers of Big Tom only serving to bind him more irrevocably to it.

Finally the big man grew tired of jeering and became sulky. He was unusually lethargic, too. Since the Loop W fiasco he hadn't led the mob out anywhere, although a few of them had pulled off little jobs of their own, with his consent, and approval of their plans of course. Sprees became more frequent and men rode into camp quarrelsome and heavy-eyed after a binge. Any other time Tom would have bawled them out, threatened them with his huge fists – 'a man who drank too much talked too much' – but now he just let it pass. The men became irritable and discontented. Without a leader they were just an aimless mob. And lately they didn't seem to have a leader ....

Some of them smuggled quantities of liquor into the valley – something that had never been done before. Then one of them, a big half-breed known as Micko, got roaring drunk just to show his independence and staggered around the camp singing at the pitch of his lungs. The rest, who weren't that drunk, watched the door of Big Tom's cabin and awaited the explosion.

There was no explosion; not right off anyway. The door opened and the Lobo leader came out. He stood in Micko's path.

'What's the matter with you?' he said.

The big half-breed was disconcerted by the simple question. He stood swaying, his narrow forehead puckered, his head on one side. He blinked. Then the Dutch courage bubbled up inside of him.

''S the boss,' he said. 'He wants ta know what's matter with me.' He thumped his chest, which was almost as wide as Tom's and said: 'I'm drunk thas whatsa matter. I'm drunk.'

Big Tom hit him coolly, square in the mouth. He did a back somersault. If he had been sober he would not have risen from that blow. Everybody was surprised that he did so. And pretty quickly too, aiming a vicious kick at the big man. His foot grazed Tom's shin.

The big Lobo went berserk. He moved like a charging grizzly. Micko did not have a chance to raise another arm or leg. He was grabbed around the waist, lifted high into the air and tossed into the midst of a bunch of his companions. They broke and he lay in a huddled heap at their feet.

Big Tom stood with his chest heaving, his tree-like arms bent, his red hair standing on end.

'Any more of yuh?' he bawled. 'Come on, I'll take all of yuh on. What's the matter with yuh – yellow?'

A daring soul spoke up: 'No, boss, we ain't yeller. but we want some action – an' fighting among ourselves ain't it.'

Big Tom's mood changed. He threw back his head and laughed.

When his mirth had subsided his words bellowed forth once more. 'Action! Action yuh want is it? I'll give you action – right now! Saddle yuh horses every one of you. It'll be dark presently. We'll ride right away.'

This was a bit too sudden for them. They weren't used to riding out on the loose as early as this. But Big Tom turned savagely on the dissenters and they shut up. They ran for their mounts. 'Four guards is all I need,' he said.

Then he suddenly spotted Mack who didn't seem in any hurry to get his horse. 'You comin'?'

'Not this time, boss,' said Mack.

Surprisingly Tom shrugged. 'Suit yourself,' he said. 'Stay with the guards.'

'All right.'

'He can take my place,' said another voice shrilly. It was Panhandle Muggins. He was climbing out of the baggy jeans he wore when doing the chores. 'It's time I got me a scalp or two,' the old man shrilled.

'So you shall, Panhandle,' said Big Tom, magnanimously. 'So you shall.'

Mack left them to it and, after collecting his Winchester, climbed the bluffs to join the four guards. Ten minutes later a wild, yelling bunch raced out of the camp. Big Tom, a huge figure mounted on his powerful stallion, was flying in front like a veritable fury unleashed.

It was well past midnight when they returned. Mack tossed away a spent cigarette, stretched his cramped muscles and went down the trail to meet them. There was no yelling now. They came on silently and slowly.

They had raided the little border town and gambling-camp of Piute Buttes, which was run by gambler Tex McCree. They had made a good haul from the casinos and honkey-tonks but hadn't been quick enough making a getaway. They had rode with sharp shooting gamblers and gunmen on their tail. They had action all right!

They left three of their number dead on the trail and brought two wounded back with them.

'It took us hours to shake the skunks off!' said one man bitterly. 'We tried to ambush 'em but nearly got surprised ourselves. It wuz a runnin' fight all the way.'

Panhandle Muggins spoke up. 'We got rid of them after

121

all tho' didn't we?' he cackled. 'That was a good move of the boss's that was – that there doublin' back. They won't find us now will they?' The old man was jubilant.

'The ol' buzzard's tasted blood,' said another man.

Big Tom was silent but he did not seem unduly perturbed about the failure of the raid. They had brought plenty of loot back with them anyway. Maybe he thought the boys had only got all they asked for.

He went immediately to his cabin.

The young lady in cowgirl costume rode slowly along the trail. In the dip below her lay the sprawling panorama of Benton City. As the girl rider drew abreast with the big old dead tree she stopped her horse. She looked around her, her full lower lip caught suddenly between small white teeth. Then as if angry with herself for pausing thus she jerked her head. She was hatless and the sudden movement made her tawny hair toss and shimmer in the sunlight. She set her lips and, looking straight ahead of her, rode slowly onwards.

Her eyes widened suddenly. A man was riding up the trail towards her. As he came nearer there was no mistaking him. He was lean and wide-shouldered, his wedge-shaped face was mahogany-tanned, his eyes seemed very keen; on his upper lip was a flowing yellow moustache which gave his face a rakishly handsome look. Locks of yellow hair flowed from beneath his tilted sombrero.

The girl looked from left to right as if seeking a place to hide and then she faced him squarely.

'Afternoon, Miss Judy,' he said.

'Good afternoon,' she replied coolly. 'I didn't expect to see you again.'

A little smile crossed the cowboy's face. 'Kind of a coincidence you should be riding past here just at this time.'

The girl's hazel eyes looked a little disconcerted.

She said: 'I was riding into town to see Doctor Greaves.'

'I called in as I passed thru'.' the young man told her. 'He was out on a case. I didn't wait. I didn't aim tuh stay in Benton City too long in case that fat sheriff came snooping.'

The girl was nonplussed. She broke the painful silence that ensued by saying: 'You're very outspoken aren't you?'

'I guess so,' he said. 'I guess I cain't help it. It's the way I've bin dragged up. If I offended I apologise.'

'You needn't,' she said.

He bowed ironically. 'Thank you, ma'am.'

The girl suddenly got tired of this verbal fencing. She flared suddenly like a fire-cracker and burst out:

'Oh, why are you such a fool? Why do you risk your neck by coming back here? There's no point .... Why do you do it? Why did you come today?'

The cowboy's facetiousness had left him. 'You know why I came, Judy,' he said softly. 'I came to see you.'

It was the first time he had used her name like that. Her face flamed hotly, her eyes widened as if she could hardly believe her ears .... The way he had spoken too...!

But her wrath, simulated or otherwise, had quickly subsided. All she could say was: 'I didn't ask you to come.'

'No, but you were here – at the time – at the place.'

The girl did not deny it. She only repeated: 'But why did you come? You can do nothing here only cause trouble and misery. My father is an old sick man. He ....'

'I wouldn't hurt anybody belonging to you,' said the man. 'I didn't come to cause trouble. I came only to see you again.'

'But what good does it do? If they tried to catch you there'd be shooting. You might get killed.'

'Would that trouble you very much?'

The girl smiled faintly. 'Well, I did nurse you back to health.'

'And made a grand job of it too.'

Yes, so that you could go back and join your friends the bandits and killers,' the girl said hotly.

Her sudden outburst silenced him for a moment. Then he said: 'They're the only friends I've ever known – apart from Doc Greaves – an' you. But, if it's any consolation to yuh, I haven't ridden with them since. And don't intend to.'

He hadn't known that himself until this very minute. But now it had tripped from his tongue he knew he meant to keep it.

'You believe me don't you?' he said.

There was no coquetry about her, despite her Eastern education. She said simply: 'Yes, I believe you.'

He said: 'And do you know why I'll never ride with them again.'

'N–no.'

'Because you've made me realise that I ain't all bad, that there's still maybe a chance for a cuss like me.'

She did not speak. He continued: 'I'd like tuh start afresh. But I guess I don't know how tuh go about it.'

Still she did not speak. Her head was bent low. The breeze blew stray tendrils of her hair over her smooth brown forehead.

'Let's ride back along apiece,' he said.

Almost mechanically she turned her horse with his and they rode along the trail away from the town, back towards the Loop W.

At the bend of the trail she suddenly said: 'You'll have to leave me now. I'll ride on to the ranch house.'

He said: 'All right. I'll be at the old tree again at the

124

same time on the third of next month.'

Her next words were hardly audible as she moved away from him. But he heard them.

'All right,' she said.

He started after her but she kicked her heels into her horse's flanks and rode like the wind.

There was a new light in the young man's eyes as he turned his horse's head and set off across the range.

He was daydreaming, he did not see the other horseman until the man was almost upon him. It was Matt Hapwood the big florid-faced straw-boss.

He said: 'Howdy, stranger.'

'Howdy,' replied Mack. He realised Hapwood did not recognise him in his face fungus.

Hapwood was quite polite. He said 'You're on private land. Do you mind if I ask you your business?'

'Jest ridin' thru',' said Mack.

Suddenly the big man's face changed, recognition flashed in his eyes. His hand moved.

His gun was tilting when Mack shot it out of his hand.

Hapwood swore and flapped the tingling fin. Then surprisingly he essayed a feeble grin.

'Gosh, you're fast!' he said.

'You're lucky, pardner,' Mack told him. 'A month or so ago I'd've shot you right between the eyes.'

Hapwood let that cryptic remark pass. He said: 'I wuz only gonna hold you up an' disarm yuh. I wanted to talk to you in comfort.'

'Talk,' said Mack. He holstered his gun.

'I've got nothin' agin you,' said Hapwood. 'What you've done or what you've been are nothin' to do with me. I know you're a good gunny an' I can allus use a good gunny.'

'You mean you're offering me a job.'

125

'Sort of.'

'What would old Maxton say about you hiring a man who'd tried to rustle his cattle.'

'Old Kit's only a figurehead. He ain't obliged to know.'

Mack was curious. 'Yeah?'

Hapwood became cagey. 'Not right now,' he said. 'I jest want to know whether I can count on you.'

'I guess so.'

'Wal, where can I reach you?'

Mack smiled: 'You'd better let me reach you,' he said. 'I'll be around again.'

'Don't make it too long,' said Hapwood. 'A month maybe.'

'All right.' Mack's manner showed he believed the strange interview was at an end.

''Mind if I get my gun?' said the big man.

Mack unsheathed his own. 'Go ahead,' he said.

Hapwood got from the saddle, retrieved his gun from the grass and holstered it. The younker watched him like a hawk.

As Hapwood remounted he said: 'You don't trust nobody do yuh?'

'Nope.'

The big man shrugged. He turned his horse. 'So long,' he called over his shoulder. Mack watched him go.

He swept the horizon with a look. Another horseman was coming across the range. Undecided, Mack waited a little. He almost gasped as the rider, galloping hard, came nearer. It was Judy Maxton.

She jerked her horse to a stop in front of him. She was panting a little. 'I heard a shot,' she said. 'What happened?'

Mack looked at the rapidly diminishing blob that was

Hapwood and his horse. Evidently the straw-boss hadn't seen Judy.

He said: 'Hapwood drew on me. I shot the gun out of his hand.'

She was angry now at giving herself away. She said: 'How clever of you. But why didn't you kill him?'

'There was no need to,' said Mack innocently.

'He knew you?'

'Oh, yes. He offered me a job.'

'*A job*! What kind of a job?'

'As far as I gathered he wanted me to carry a gun for him. But how, when or where I don't know.'

The girl looked startled. 'What did you tell him?'

'I told him I'd think it over.'

Her face was clouded now as well as puzzled. She didn't look at him. She said: 'You'd better ride. He might bring the men after you.' She tried to sound light-hearted: 'I'll have to be getting back before Dad sends a search-party out after me.'

'I'm going,' he said.

He kneed his horse forward and grabbed her hand. She did not pull it away. He said: 'Everything's all right isn't it?'

She brightened. 'Certainly. Only Hapwood's a queer man. I don't like him. I wish Dad would get rid of him. He's treacherous – he was trying to trap you.'

'Well, he didn't, so there's nothing to worry about.'

She snatched her hand away. 'I must go.' Again she felt him staring as she sped away. Gosh she could ride. She was no milk-and-white Eastern filly. She was a Westerner to the core .... She'd make a grand wife for any Western man ....

His own harsh laugh in the silence made him jump. These were crazy thoughts to come into the mind of an owl-hooter.

127

# CHAPTER TEN

When he got back to the camp of the Loboes things were quiet. Most of the men were gambling around a slow fire in the morning sunshine. They greeted him desultorily.

Mack fed his horse then went to the bunkhouse and lay on his back on his cot. He smoked and dreamed a little. He was like that when the banging of the cookhouse pan and cries of the time honoured phrase, 'Come an' get it' awoke the valley echoes.

Mack's belly answered and he joined the throng for the cookhouse. He saw Johnny Lee, the Chinese cook, carry a tray of food to Big Tom's cabin, knock on the door and go inside. So the wolf was laying-low in his den.

Only the Lobo leader knew the purpose of Mack's trips. But the younker knew most of the men were mighty curious. As he took a seat by the long deal table a few of them tossed jocularly-innocent enquiries at him. Had he brought any scalps back with him? How many banks had he knocked over? …. One man gave him quite a start by saying: 'When yuh gonna marry that dark-eyed senorita, sucker?' Then he realised a lot of them must think he'd been on the prod somewhere with one of the notorious ladies of the border-towns. He parried their thrusts good-

128

humouredly. Pretty soon the gabbing died down and all that could be heard was the champing of jaws and occasional cries for further utensils or condiments.

After the meal Mack was crossing to the bunkhouse to get his 'makings' when he met Big Tom. The latter did not halt, he just nodded and said: 'You're back then?'

'Yeh, I'm back.'

'Fine,' said the big man.

A couple of minutes later Mack saw him ride out of the camp. He sat his big stallion superbly, a wild, commanding figure of a man. But what a queer moody case he was – like the night winds across the prairies, first blowing warm, then cold.

The men around the camp-fire were wrangling: many of them figured it was time they had another crack at Tex McCree's gambler's stronghold, Piute Buttes, and avenge the drubbing they had received last time and the death of their three comrades.

'What d'you think, Mack?' called one of them.

'Wal, I wasn't in on that shindig,' the yellow-haired younker replied. 'So I cain't work up no bile about it.'

'That's right, he wasn't,' said somebody else.

'How come?' said another one.

Mack ignored the query and said: 'What's the boss say about it?'

'Nobody asked him. But we aim tuh.'

'I reckin you'll come along this time, Mack?' said another one.

'I reckin not!'

This decisive answer nonplussed the questioners but they mumbled among themselves. Mack noted that his old pard, Panhandle was one of the gang nearest the fire. Since the old man's part in the Piute Buttes raid he had

129

ceased to be looked upon by most as merely the daffy old coot who did the chores and helped with the cooking and was becoming almost 'one of the boys', He was never tired of recounting, with much vituperation , expectoration and embellishment, his exploits when young. A bunch of the younger men were gathered around him now egging him on. Although they joshed him, his tales of Geronimo, Billy the Kid, Sam Bass and the James boys fired their blood-thirsty imagination.

None of the Loboes except maybe the guards saw their leader return. But his horse was back in the stables the following day and his meals were taken to the cabin by Johnny Lee. The big man kept himself out of sight.

The following day he appeared at his door when Mack was passing nearby and called him in.

The cabin was a stout two-roomed affair furnished with handmade chairs, a table, a big cupboard and a small book-case which was packed to overflowing with dusty leather volumes, incongruous in such a setting. They were relics of Tom Heineman's other life, probably he had not opened them for years. Mack knew the other room contained only a cot, a chair and a small bedside table with a hurricane lantern upon it. The camp had been built by the first members of the band who now called themselves the Loboes, men as old or older than Tom. Many of them were dead now, very few by natural causes, while the others still rode with the bunch. Most of the furniture, according to Panhandle, had been made by an outlaw called 'Chips' Lockmore, who had been a ship's carpenter before he came West. He had been killed by a ranger about three years ago.

'Sit down, Mack,' said the Lobo leader.

Mack sat down. He rolled himself a quirly and handed the 'makings' across.

They lit up, then Tom said: 'Did yuh see Doc Greaves again?'

'Nope. He was out.'

'Did you see the gel?'

'Yeh.'

'Any trouble while you were there? Did you get spotted or anything?' Mack told him of his meeting with Matt Hapwood. When he had finished the big man snorted. 'You ought to've plugged him.'

'Maybe I had.'

'I'm fixin' for a jamboree tonight, Mack,' said Tom. 'Another raid on Piute Buttes. The boys are rarin' to go. Are you comin' along?'

'No, Tom. Not ever again I guess.'

For a second the big man's eyes narrowed. He was unused to such bluff retaliation. Then his face cleared. He leaned forward and pressed a huge hand on Mack's knee.

'Suit yourself, son,' he said. 'I guess it's for the best at that.'

'You figured it that way yourself a few days back.'

'Yeh, guess I did. Anyway, will you tell the boys what I told you? Tell 'em to be ready tonight.'

'Yeh, I'll do that,' said Mack. He rose and left the cabin.

He went to the few men at the fire first. They greeted the news jubilantly. The smaller bunkhouse was empty except for a big gunny who lay on his bunk moaning like a child. He was sick with dysentery.

Mack went to the larger bunkhouse. Two card games were in full swing. There were lookers-on too, the place was packed, the air blue and shifting with cigarette smoke.

Mack stood just inside the door and yelled: 'Hold it a mite, boys. I got somethin' to tell yuh!'

The buzz of conversation died down. 'What goes on?'

131

'I've jest seen the boss. He's got a shindig planned for tonight. Piute Buttes.'

Reception of this news was mixed. 'Aw, hell,' groaned one man. 'An' I'd got the best run of luck for years.'

'It's what most of yuh wanted,' said Mack.

'You goin'?' said somebody.

'Nope. Not this time.'

Old Panhandle bobbed up suddenly and stood in front of the yellow-haired young man.

'What's the matter, Mack,' he croaked. 'Yaller?'

There was dead silence. Then Mack grinned. 'Quit blowin', old-timer,' he said.

'Blowin' am I?' shrilled Panhandle coming nearer. 'I never missed a raid till the boss made me. Lookee here!' He suddenly whipped his shirt tails from out of his trousers, wrenched his shirt up until it was in folds around his neck. His yellow, skinny body was pockmarked with red scars. He turned around. His back was the same.

'Look at them!' he said. 'Wounds! An' I'm proud of 'em.'

'You bin lucky, Panhandle,' said Mack softly.

The old man whirled, dropping his shirt. 'Pah!' he said.

He spat. The white globule landed on the toe of Mack's boot. The old man turned again and walked away, his shirt tails flapping.

'He is yaller,' said somebody else. 'He took all that.'

The speaker rose. He was a white-faced beanpole of a guy called Slash who carried a perpetual chip on his shoulder.

'You make noises, Slash,' said Mack mildly.

'Yeh?' said the beanpole belligerently. He drew himself up to his full six-feet four and strode forward.

Mack changed the position of his feet. Instinctively

132

Slash raised his hands. Mack's right arm curled out. The fist exploded in the thin man's midriff. He doubled over like a jacknife. Mack's left straightened him up again. Then the right came over, driving full into the middle of his face.

The men scattered as Slash's long length cut like a scythe through them. He took a table with him, turning it right over, and finished up draped very awkwardly around one of its upturned legs. He was out to the wide.

'I take lip from ol' men,' said Mack. 'But from nobody else.'

'Be ready to ride tonight,' he added as he left the cabin.

That night, up on the bluffs, he watched them ride out madly with Big Tom at their head. In the starlight the Lobo leader looked huge and fearsome. He was a different man to the quiet, chatty one of the afternoon. He rode as if a demon possessed him. For the first time Mack had a fuller realisation of Tom Heineman's tragedy: that demon was always with him inwardly now, gnawing at him, it was only at times like this that he could let it loose and, for a spell, satiate its inexorable lust. He was not a man now, he was a rampaging devil.

When he returned, ten hours later, he was a raving madman. And the remains of his followers were bloody, broken men. Piute Buttes was their Jinx.

They had run into a strong bunch of Texas Rangers who had been ranging that area. They fought with an even chance until the townsfolk of the Buttes streamed out and joined forces with the law. The outlaws scattered and ran for it. Many were killed, others had gotten split off from the main band and lost. And the posse, which now outnumbered them three to one were right on the tail of Big Tom and his band.

133

The big man was cursing and raving horribly. 'We'll hold 'em off from here,' he roared. 'Get all the rifles an' ammunition up here.'

But it was already too late. The posse was coming up the pass. They began to shoot. The weary, beaten outlaws broke and ran. They knew the hills better than anybody, like fleeing rats they sought holes in which to hide.

Big Tom raved and called them 'yeller skunks' and worse. He turned in his saddle, and grinning fiendishly blazed away at the oncoming riders.

Mack rode up to him. 'Tom, yuh crazy fool!' he yelled. 'Come on, it's your only chance.'

The big man turned on him, his eyes blazing; he was mouthing but Mack could not hear what he said above the deafening blatter of gunfire. Slugs were hissing perilously close.

Mack whipped out a .45. 'Come on,' he snarled. He hit Tom's mount a sharp blow across the rump with the barrel of the gun.

The horse bounded forward and began to gallop at breakneck speed along the treacherous trail. It's rider could not stop it. All he could do was hang on. Even Mack's powerful beast could not keep up with them. As for the posse, they were on unfamiliar, dangerous ground and had to go carefully. They were soon outdistanced.

The camp was in an uproar. Many men were trying to salvage what they could of their belongings and, particularly, their 'cache'. Somebody tipped a lamp over – accidentally or purposely. Pretty soon the bunkhouse was a raging inferno. The fire began to spread.

Big Tom's stallion, now as berserk as his master, sped across the clearing and into the hills beyond. Mack kept close behind them. About half-a-dozen of the men joined up with him. A rifle spoke and the rearmost one fell and found his last resting-place in the valley of the Loboes.

The following day, beneath a broiling noonday sun, seven dirty, weary riders crossed the border into Mexico. They consisted of Big Tom Heineman, Mack Danvers, Panhandle Muggins and four others.

The days, the weeks were dull and lethargic, passing lead-enly with the hot Mexican sun and the sand, the sordid hideouts, the bad food, and the *tequila* that made a man brave and new again for a while then plunged him into the very depths of misery. But it was a cool Texan night with the stars like twinkling jewels when Mack Danvers pushed open the door of Doc Greaves place in Benton City and went inside.

He was leaner, his moustache was ragged and his face had a gaunt wolfish look. Greaves did not recognise him until he spoke.

'My eyes ain't so good lately, Mack,' he apologized. 'You've changed – and I guess I never expected to see you again.'

'I waited for Judy yesterday,' said Mack. 'She didn't come.'

The doctor looked leaner and worried-looking too. He shook his white head.

'She didn't expect you, son. We heard Big Tom an' his Loboes had been driven from the States – a lot of 'em wiped out. We thought you were either dead or hiding-out somewhere.'

'An' I guess you didn't care a whole lot, anyway,' said Mack bitterly.

'We cared,' said the doc simply. 'Both of us. But Judy's in trouble. Her dad's dead.'

'Dead?'

'Yes. His chair tipped up comin' down the verandah steps. I always said they were too high. Broke his neck.' The doc's words came out in a rush. 'That poker-faced man of his was pushing the chair. He reckoned he slipped, and let it go. But I don't think it was an accident – it was all planned. Matt Hapwood's taken over up there now. He's got all that mob of treacherous gunnies solid behind him. Judy can't do a thing in her own ranch. She's stickin' ....'

'But how about the law, the sheriff, what's he doin'?'

'He can't do nothin'. I went up there with him and some deputies. Matt Hapwood turned us off, said we had no rights, he was second-in-command, he'd taken over now the boss was dead. We couldn't do nothing, we were surrounded by gunmen, outnumbered four to one.'

'But can't you get a posse? – the townsfolk, surely there's enough ....'

'No, Mack, the townsfolk won't meddle. Some of 'em are even crowing over it. They don't know Judy. To them she's just old Kit's daughter – and Kit was hated plenty.'

'But Hapwood can't do it .... It's the craziest stick-up I've ever heard of ....'

'But pretty foolproof in this territory. Old Kit took the land from the Indians. If Judy leaves altogether Hapwood can take over entirely.'

'If he touches Judy ....'

'He doesn't. He just lets her be. She's in the house on her own. Nobody goes near her. She's got nobody. He hopes to scare her out like that .... I went there .... Look,' the doctor rolled up his sleeve. Round his forearm was a vivid red weal.

'Hapwood snaked me with a stock whip and pulled me

136

from my horse. He made me walk home and said if I went there again he'd let the boys get to work on me .... I'm an old man, Mack. I can't do nothing!' The last sentence was like a cry of agony.

'No, that's right, doc.' Mack hitched up his gunbelt, his eyes shining queerly. 'I'll go see Judy,' he said.

Doc Greaves opened his mouth as if to expostulate, then closed it again, and rose from his chair.

'I'm comin' with you.'

'No you're not,' said Mack roughly. 'You're staying here. You'll be better off here.'

The doctor's eyes dropped before the fire in the other man's. He sank into his chair again like an old tired man.

Mack Danvers rode out on to the range. He was not crazy enough to ride down the trail to the Loop W. He made a wide detour and came out by the corral behind the ranch house.

There was a light in an upstairs window, the window of the room next to the one Mack had occupied when he lay wounded. The light was the only sign of life except for the three horses standing silently in the corner of the corral.

Mack figured that at this time of night, all the men who were not riding herd would be in their own quarters. He remembered how bumpy the wall beneath his window had been, how Big Tom had climbed up there. He tied his horse to a bar of the corral fence and ran lightly across the hard dirt-ground.

He paused a moment, looking up at the darkened window, then at the next one lit-up but curtained. Then he reached up and found a couple of handholds and began to climb.

His hands grasped the window-sill. He hauled himself up. He groped at the sash then realised it was tightly shut.

Clinging perilously with one hand, he reached with the other into his tattered jeans and drew forth the long, thin-bladed clasp knife he always carried. He jabbed at the sash with this and tried to prise it open. The arm he hung on with began to ache, sweat began to break out on his forehead.

He succeeded in inserting the knife. He felt for the catch, found it, and sighed with relief as he managed to force it back. Now he could get his fingers in. He raised the window and climbed into the room.,

'Stay right where you are,' said a sharp voice. 'Raise your hands or I'll shoot.'

Mack raise his hands just in case. He recognised that voice. He said: 'It's me, Judy – Mack.'

He saw the shadowy figure in the doorway start. The barrel of the gun gleamed as it jumped in her hand.

'I wish you'd quit pointin' that thing at me,' said Mack. 'It makes me nervous.'

She lowered it. He crossed the room towards her and she moved into the passage. Still she did not speak.

She backed into the lighted room, the door of which was half-open. He followed her.

There she dropped the heavy Colt on the bed. She sagged. He started forward and caught her in his arms. He held her for a moment, leaning against him, her head upon his chest. Then she looked up. 'I'm all right now,' she said. 'Reaction. I nearly dropped when I heard your voice. I – I never thought I'd hear it again.'

Her eyes were very soft and bright. Mack felt kind of giddy himself. His head drooped over hers. Their lips met.

Afterwards she clung to him, trembling a little, her head buried in his shirt front. Her voice was muffled.

'Mack – I could hardly believe it was you. But now I

138

know it is. I know ....' It was sweet nonsense. Mack stroked her tawny hair, soft as silk beneath his palm

'It's me all right, *chiquita*. You haven't got to worry. You're never gonna lose me again.'

When they were a little more rational they sat side by side on the bed – now was no time for conventionalities – and she tried to tell him coherently the story of her father's death. He made it easier for her by divulging the fact that he had already heard most of it from Doc Greaves. She could do no more but answer a few questions.

'They haven't harmed me,' she said. 'They keep away from me. I have to prepare my own food and everything. Supplies are left outside the backdoor every morning .... But – but Matt Hapwood scares me. I'm more frightened of him than anything on earth. He prowls around at night. I think he'd try to get in if he wasn't afraid of his men finding out. That's why I keep the gun. I found it in Dad's drawer – and plenty of ammunition. I thought you were Hapwood. If you had not spoken I think I would've pressed the trigger.'

An icy choking feeling rose in Mack's breast, a feeling he had not felt for a couple of months or more. The lust to kill, to get another human being in front of his spouting guns and blast him from the face of the earth.

This reaction was replaced, almost as suddenly, by cold logic and a plan began to form in his mind.

'Listen, Judy,' he said and began to talk.

When he had finished she caught hold of him again, clung to him.

'No, Mack, it's too risky. You mustn't do it. They might – they might kill you.'

'No, they wouldn't do that, Judy. It's a chance, a big

chance. Maybe it's our only chance. I've got to do it.'

Finally she knew it was useless to argue any longer. She capitulated. They rose. One last kiss then he left. He quitted the house by the same way he had entered it.

He mounted his horse and set him at a gallop, making right for the buildings which housed the herds.

The door of the long log bunkhouse was flung open, spilling light, making the black earth into shimmering silver. A man came out.

'Somebody's makin' a helluva racket,' he shouted. 'Who is it?'

'Where can I find Matt Hapwood?' yelled Mack.

The man drew his gun. He was fast. Old Kit Maxton had picked his men well.

'A stranger,' said the gunny. Another man joined him. 'What do you want with Matt Hapwood?' said the second one.

'That's my business,' Mack told them. 'But he'll be expectin' me. Where is he?'

'Better take him, George,' said the second man. 'But keep him covered.'

George nodded his head. 'Light down, stranger,' he said. 'I'll be watchin' yuh.'

Carefully Mack dismounted from his horse. 'Straight ahead,' said George. Mack led his horse with him.

They halted outside a small log cabin raised on piles with five wooden steps leading up to its closed door. Chinks of light shone through a curtain in the window at the side.

The cautious George went up the steps sideways with his gun pointing at Mack's head.

'Hold it still,' said the latter. 'It might go off.'

George rapped at the door with the knuckles of his free hand.

'Come in,' said a voice. George opened the door. 'I got a stranger here, boss, who wants tuh see yuh.'

'Bring him in.'

George jerked his head. He opened the door wide. Mack climbed the steps and passed in front of him and into the interior of the cabin. It was rigged up untidily like an office. Hapwood was sitting in a half-backed swivel chair before a huge roll-top desk. He was half-turned towards the door.

Another man sat on a chair beside the desk. He was young and mean-looking. He had his chair tilted back on two legs. On his knee was a black, shiny forty-five with a mother-of-pearl handle. He was polishing the gun with an oily rag. His black, button-like eyes bored into Mack.

'Oh, it's you,' said Hapwood at length.

George turned to leave. 'Close the door an' stay here, George,' said Hapwood.

'All right, boss,' George hefted his gun in his hand. Mack turned his back on him.

'I came after that job you offered me, Mr Hapwood,' he said. 'I came in peace and I don't like guns held on me.'

Hapwood grinned. Then he turned to the man at his side. 'That him?'

'That's him,' said the young man. He elevated his gun and pointed it at Mack's chest. 'I just loaded it,' he said.

'What's the idea?' said Mack as George's hands reached out and took his guns.

Hapwood leaned forward. His voice dripped with venom when he spoke. 'You came for a job!' he jeered. 'You came to spy you mean.' He jerked his thumb at the younger man beside him. 'Jack here saw you comin' out of Doc Greaves' office tonight. He follered you but lost you out on the range – the skunk was drunk I guess.' A faint

141

smile crossed the young man's poker face.

'I figured you'd turn up here sooner or later,' concluded Hapwood.

Mack grinned. 'You got me all wrong,' he said. 'I did visit the doc, yeh. He was moaning about the death of ol' Kit and the way things wuz bein' run here. As soon as I could get away from him I made for here. I made a detour, 'cos I'm kinda cautious, an' came in the back way. This seems like a dandy set-up for me, I'm with yuh all the way if you'll have me.'

'Yeah?' said Hapwood. His eyes shifted; there was a movement behind Mack; he threw himself sideways. The descending gun-barrel grazed his shoulder. Mack caught the man's arm, swinging him in front, a human shield. Young Jack rose swiftly, gun ready. In that split second Mack had got hold of George's gun. He pressed the trigger.

Jack grunted horribly, doubling up, his own gun speaking. George screamed and crumpled as a bullet smashed his kneecap. Matt Hapwood dived across the body of his young *segunda*.

His bullet head hit Mack in the middle; he went down with Hapwood on top of him. The big man's left hand grasped his gun-wrist.

Mack jerked up his knees. Hapwood's grip slackened. Mack brought the gun round. Then Hapwood opened his mouth and yelled for help.

Mack hit him twice, savagely with the gun-barrel. Hapwood went limp, the side of his head a bloody mess. Mack pushed him out of the way, opened the door. He fired random shots at running figures then took a flying leap from the second step to his horse's saddle. The horse bounded forward, he knew when to hasten. A few shots winged after them as they sped away.

# CHAPTER ELEVEN

Mack rode in a wide half-circle and made for Benton City. He figured the folks who were hunting him wouldn't think he'd have the nerve to go back there. However, to be on the safe side, he parked his horse behind Doc Greaves' place this time. He rapped the door, opened it and walked in.

The doc was sitting opposite the door; half-turned towards it was a portly man with a black walrus moustache. A star glittered on his breast. Clem Poynton, sheriff – and reaching for his gun.

'Hold it, Clem,' said the doc. 'Mack's a friend.'

'He hadn't useter be,' said Poynton dryly. His eyes were mighty sharp. 'I ain't forgot yuh, young feller,' he said. 'Even if you have changed, an' growed that stuff on your lip.' Half unconsciously he stroked his own luxuriant growth. 'Good job Doc's rootin' fer yuh,' he growled.

Mack grinned at his scowl and perched himself on the edge of the desk.

'I'm glad to see yuh back all in one piece anyway,' said Greaves.

'I nearly wasn't ....' Mack told them what had happened.

When he had finished the sheriff said reflectively: 'They

really mean business don't they? .... If I could only get enough men together to go and have a real crack at 'em.'

'I've been doin' some figurin',' said Mack. 'If you'll scout around an' get as many men as you can I'll do the rest.'

'The rest of what?' snorted Sheriff Poynton.

'I cain't tell you much about it now. I gotta ride. I'll be back in a couple o' days.'

'No, yuh don't,' said the sheriff. Then his mouth dropped open. He was looking into the muzzle of Mack's gun.

'Don't be silly, sheriff,' the yellow-haired man said. 'I guess you haven't worked over him enough, doc.'

'I guess not. I'll start rootin' again, Mack.'

The young man backed to the door. 'Like I said, I'll be back in a coupla days an', if you really want to help Judy, and get the ranch back for her I hope you'll have all the men you can get, ready to be called into action.'

He dodged through the door and slammed it behind him. As he galloped off the door opened again. The voice of Sheriff Poynton bawled: 'Come back, yuh young skunk.' But there were no shots.

Maybe it was only a coincidence that a couple of days later two strangers were picked up roaming across Loop W range. They submitted meekly to being disarmed by Hapwood's gunnies and led to the ranch house.

One of them was a huge man with flaming red beard and, incongruously, cheap steel-rimmed spectacles. He said he couldn't see tuh shoot straight without them.

His companion was a wizened oldster with a straggling goatee beard and a habit of cackling suddenly and harshly and for no obvious reason.

144

They were tattered grimy saddle-tramps. Their horses were flea-bitten nags. The only clean thing about both men's outfit was their shiny low-slung guns. The four Loop W gunfighters who picked them up exchanged significant glances; they knew the signs.

They paraded the two men in front of Hapwood who had his head and one side of his face swathed in bandages and was as touchy as a bronc with a burr under its saddle.

The red-bearded man strode forward. The oldster shuffled along a little way behind.

One of the Loop W riders said: 'We picked these bozoes up out on the range, boss. They say they're looking for jobs.'

'What kinds of jobs?' growled Hapwood.

The red-bearded giant spoke up: 'Anythin' on a ranch, suh. Anythin' atall. An' my pard here is a mighty fine cook.'

'You don't say,' sneered Hapwood. 'He looks no good atall tuh me.'

'No good, he says!' cackled the oldster. He drew alongside his big pardner and shook a bony fist at Hapwood. 'Tell me tuh do somethin'. Anythin'.'

'You're crazy.' Hapwood turned to the red-beard once more. 'You can do anything on a ranch can yuh? Can yuh shoot?'

'Yes, suh. If one o' your boys will give me my guns back I'll show yuh.'

The Loop W ramrod hesitated for a moment. Then he said: 'Give him his guns. Keep him covered. Any funny business, mister, an' you're a dead pigeon.'

'I ain't aimin' tuh commit suicide, suh,' said red-beard as he took his guns and holstered them.

He turned away from the assembled company, stood

slackly immobile for a moment, facing a picket fence. Then he blurred into action. Both guns were out and blazing. They stopped as suddenly, simultaneously: there was no raggedness.

Red-beard slid them into their sheaths. 'Fourth post from the end,' he said. 'There's a circle of six shots in the top of it.' It was a very thin post.

One of the Loop W men strode forward and scrutinized the oval top

'He's right, boss, a perfect circle. Some shootin'!'

Hapwood turned to the old man, sneeringly: 'And you, pop. Can you shoot?'

'Can I shoot? Gimme my gun. Gimme my gun.'

'Is he safe?' said Hapwood, innocently, to red-beard.

'Yeh, he's safe. He's just a little cantankerous. Give him his gun.'

Hapwood jerked his head. One of the men handed a gun over.

The oldster did not sheath it. 'I'm kinda stiff an' I cain't draw like I useter,' he said. 'But I kin shoot. Gimme a target.'

The big ramrod gazed around him. Then he said: 'See the fence there your pardner shot at?'

'Yeh.'

'Halfway down the – er – eighth post there's a round black mark, a splotch o' mud or somethin' .... See it?'

The oldster peered. 'Yeh, I see it.'

'Pip that, dead centre.'

The old man raised his gun, took aim and fired. One of the waddies ran forward and looked at the post. 'Yeh,' he said. 'Almost plumb centre.'

'Not bad for an old jackass,' said Hapwood, grinning. 'Better take his gun off him again boys.'

The old man snorted as he handed the weapon over.

Hapwood said: 'Where do you men come from?'

'Up in the Pecos,' said red-beard. 'Last job we had was with an outfit called themselves the Cross Bar Seven.'

'Why did you leave 'em?'

'Purty crummy outfit. Besides we like travellin'. Figured we'd get another job in this territory. Better land. A big outfit like this is jest what we're lookin' for. We're fed up of crummy little outfits. All we want is a trial, suh, we'll give satisfaction. Anythin' you say 'ull go with us.'

'That's how it'd hafta be – an' no questions,' said Hapwood harshly. 'Your names?'

'I'm Sid Boyton,' said red-beard.

'We'll jest call yuh Red.'

The big man shrugged. 'They most do, suh,' he said.

The oldster said: 'My name's Nick Lannigan; call me Abe.'

'They call him that fer Abe Lincoln,' said red-beard. 'Cos he's kinda cantankerous an' outspoken. He's as gentle as a dove really.'

'If I set you on, Mr Nick called Abe,' said Hapwood jocularly, 'I don't want yuh causin' any trouble. You go trouble-makin' on'y when I say so … savvy?'

'You're the boss,' said Abe, quite meekly.

Hapwood turned again to Red. 'Do you hafta wear them glasses?'

'Yes, suh. I'm kinda short-sighted. But with these I guess I can see better'n the next man."

'All right,' said the ramrod. 'I'll give yuh a trial – both of yuh. If you pull your weight an' do as you're told – no matter what – you'll be in. If not, you'll be out on your ears, pronto …. I'm goin' ridin' now. I'll see you when I come back.' He turned to one of the men. 'Take them an' give them some chow. Find 'em a bunk apiece.'

The ranny led the way. 'Thank you, suh,' said Red as he and his old pard turned to follow.

Hapwood watched them go. Then he turned to the others. 'They look just the type we want,' he said. 'But keep an eye on 'em. It don't do tuh take any chances.'

But the two new men proved themselves to be good and amiable rannies – except that Abe had an altercation with the cook … then mollified that worthy, a fat simpleton, by showing him a new way to do blackberry pie.

Mack Danvers, Doc Greaves and Sheriff Poynton sat around the table beneath the lamp in the doctor's room. The sheriff was speaking: 'I'll play along with yuh young man,' he said. 'The doc's talked me into it …. But I ain't promising anything mind you. I don't know who your two friends up at the ranch are but I got my suspicions. I ain't promising anything to any of yuh.'

'We'll worry about that when the job's done,' said Mack. 'If we haggle too much among ourselves now the job'll never get done. Are all your men ready?'

'Ready an' waitin',' said the sheriff. 'When does the balloon go up?'

'About midnight tonight. Get your men ready about 11.30 outside town.'

'They'll be there.'

'An' remember to look out for my pards. I don't want 'em shot by our own side. You can't mistake 'em. One's a big red-bearded fellow, the other an oldtimer with a goatee.'

'Big Red-beard,' eh?' said the sheriff. He exchanged glances with the doc, who didn't say a word.

'I gotta get ridin',' said Mack hastily. 'I'll see yuh later.'

Doc rose and shook him by the hand. 'Good luck son.'

The sheriff stuck his paw out awkwardly but he didn't say anything. Mack shook it, left them quickly.

At about that time Red and Abe were taking it easy in the big bunkhouse at the Loop W. They had done a full day's work now and acquitted themselves well. They had also been accepted by the 'boys' – particularly Abe, the oldster, with his fund of tall stories. He had just finished one and, oblivious of the badinage tossed at him from all sides, was deftly rolling himself a smoke.

It was getting late, everybody began to loll and have that last couple of smokes. Many of them were already yawning. One by one they began to turn in.

Ten minutes later the second of the big hurricane-lanterns was doused and the bunkhouse was enveloped in darkness. There were choruses of 'good-nights'.

Pretty soon all that could be heard was the sounds of sleep: the deep gentle breathing, the fat man snoring in the corner, the young ranny who mumbled, the snuffler and the whistler. They were all there: the queer noises of sleeping, work-tired men.

An hour passed, a slice of unconsciousness to the log-like humans in their narrow bunks. A huge shadow rose like a phantom from the floor and was joined by a smaller, thinner form. The two of them began to flit around the cabin.

A man growled as a hand reached above his head, taking the gunbelt from its hook. There was a swish, a dull thud. Then the silence of the familiar sounds closed over again.

The door opened and two bulky figures slid out. 'Drop 'em down over there,' hissed the big one. 'Have you got the rope?'

149

'Yeh,' the smaller one followed him. The guns in their arms glinted, the gunbelts that festooned them. They parked the lot in a clump of grass about two hundred yards from the bunkhouse door.

'Quickly,' hissed the big man. The other one handed him a riata. He tied the end of another one to it as they went back to the door.

He coiled them. He tied the end of the coil to the stout half-hoop handle of the door. Then he began to walk around the cabin, playing out the rope.

His companion remained by the door, a gun in his hand.

Sounds of movement came from inside the bunkhouse. Both men, one at the front the other now at the back, froze; the latter drew his gun too. The sounds died down.

Presently the big man joined the other at the door again. He had ringed the hut tightly all round with the rope. He still had plenty of slack. He began to repeat the process, barring the door and both the windows with tough, taut, rawhide.

As he returned the second time, still with loose coils around his arm, he said: 'I guess it's safe to make sure o' them guns now, Panhandle.'

'All right, Tom.' The old man went across to the piled guns and began to take out their shells, to transfer them to his own belt and to the pouches in his jeans.

Presently the big man joined him. 'All tied up like a box of chocolates,' he said. 'I've knotted the end up like nobody's business. They'll have a job to break thru' that.' He began to collect ammunition himself.

They worked fast. 'Let's get moving,' said the big man. Gun in hand, he led the way.

Over in a room in the big empty ranch house, Judy

Maxton stirred uneasily in her sleep. Then she sat up suddenly in bed, her hand reaching beneath her pillow. With the big Colt clenched in her fist she listened. She heard the stealthy sounds again. She rose swiftly and silently and donned her dressing-gown. Then, the gun held in front of her, she crept from the room and along the passage.

The next door was slightly ajar. She pushed it open.

'Judy,' whispered a voice. She could not mistake it. Or the tall lean figure. She had known that some day he would come again through that window which she had left ajar night after night since that first one.

'Mack,' she breathed and ran to him.

He took the gun gently from her and drew her to him.

# CHAPTER TWELVE

Big Tom and Panhandle ran to the stables. The big simple stable-youth woke up. He did not lack guts, or foolhardiness. Even though they had him covered he dragged at his Colt. Big Tom slashed him across the side of the head with a gun-barrel.

'He'll rest awhile,' he said. 'I'll drag him out.'

He pulled the unconscious youth out on to the hard sod of the yard. Meanwhile, Panhandle was chasing out the horses.

Lights went on in the bunkhouse. There was a chorus of shouts. Panhandle put a match to the dry straw of the stables. It flared. He ran round, spreading the fire.

Then he came out. 'I'll see to them bozoes,' he said.

'Right,' said Tom. 'I'll carry on.'

They separated. Panhandle ran back to the bunkhouse and stationed himself against a water butt in the shelter of the fence opposite. He wasn't taking any chances. Maybe some of the boys in there still had guns cached away someplace.

He triggered both his .45s, sending the slugs screaming high, smashing the top halves of the windows. Inside a man cried out with pain.

The clamour died. Panhandle shouted: 'Listen, you skunks. You'd better keep away from the doors an' windows. Lie low or you're liable to get kilt....'

The voices clamoured again. 'What's the game?' yelled a single stentorian one.

For answer Panhandle fired again, emptying his guns.

Silence fell once more. As he reloaded the old man broke it by yelling: 'I mean business. I'm gonna keep shooting an' I got enough ammunition here to last me a year. Don't think you can make a break – my pardners are all around.'

The door of the bunkhouse shook as somebody battered at it from inside. Panhandle fired once, deliberately.

There was a choking cry. Silence, then a voice said, 'You've killed a man.'

Panhandle began to cackle. 'I'll kill a damsight more of yuh if you don't behave yourselves.'

He stopped laughing. The voices inside were subdued. Suddenly the boom of an old Sharps rifle split the night apart. Panhandle began to cackle again as a slug chipped the top of the water-butt behind which he squatted. Even though he had them hog-tied he had been too canny to come out in the open. Somebody had evidently dug the rifle up from someplace. He'd let them waste their ammunition.

The Sharps boomed five more times. It was evidently the only weapon they had. The man could shoot; he knew roughly where Panhandle lay too; some of the slugs hit the barrel but failed to go right through the rainwater that filled it almost to the brim. Panhandle was cackling all the time. The men in the bunkhouse however, together with their gun were making too much noise to be able to hear him.

The shooting stopped but the voices didn't. Panhandle's sharp old ears caught the words. 'Maybe you got him.'

He poked one of his guns around the water-butt and emptied it into the windows.

The yelling that ensued was fiendish. A man screamed in pain and rage. Another one bawled: 'You madman! What's your game? What do you want?'

Panhandle's only answer was more shrill laughter. Thought him mad did they? He'd play up to that. He'd put the fear of death into 'em. And death itself too if they tried any games.

As the shooting began Tom Heineman lurked outside Matt Hapwood's sleeping quarters. He knew that in the adjoining buildings were the cook, a couple of odd job men and the gunny the big ramrod always kept around as a sort of bodyguard. Mack Danvers had killed one of these bodyguards but Hapwood had no difficulty in selecting another one from his crew.

The stables and feed-barn were crackling merrily, the flames shooting high. They would be seen for miles around. Big Tom hoped the right people got here first. The night was like ruddy daylight. The flames ate up timber and grass, travelling swiftly. If the folks didn't start to come out soon they'd get roasted. Save Tom a job ....

He sought cover as a man came out of the buildings. He came off the verandah and began to run across the glare of the clearing towards the bunkhouse. That would not do! But even Big Tom Heineman could not shoot a man in the back. He shot him in the leg then, as he tried to rise gun in hand, shot him again in the shoulder.

The fat cook came out on the verandah, a shotgun in

154

his hand. Tom fired again. The cook squealed and staggered. The gun flew from his grasp. He held his dripping, shattered hand in front of him, his eyes agonized and wide in the fire-glare.

Tom covered the intervening space in three bounds. The cook mouthed at him as if pleading for mercy. Hardly pausing in his stride Tom swung his gun. The cook went down before the steel arc and rolled to the bottom of the steps.

Tom collided with another man who came rushing from the doorway. They wrestled, grappling for each other's guns. But the other man was speedily a puppet in the hands of this berserker giant. He was lifted and thrown with such force against the verandah rail that it caved. The body rolled in the dirt of the yard then lay still.

Tom heard movements and flattened himself against the wall beside the door. He was only just in time, for slugs cut a swathe in the air as the double-blatter of Colts came from inside.

Then there was dead silence as Tom waited. He knew there were only two more men left to deal with. But they were the two most dangerous: Matt Hapwood and his pet gunny. That was probably the gunny in there. Hapwood hadn't shown himself yet. He was probably lurking back there by his sleeping quarters.

Tom was in a ticklish position and he knew it. His berserker rage had died and he felt ice-cold and deadly competent. The added hidden menace of Hapwood, on top of the waiting gunman in there, lent a piquant flavour to this escapade. Tom realised that, for the first time in many years, he was really enjoying himself. Maybe it was because he was fighting for something good for a change.

A board creaked inside the house. Still Tom waited.

The flames were licking at the end of the building now. Whoever it was in there, pretty soon he'd have to come a-running. Tom heard the sound of Panhandle's Colts. Every now and then there was the familiar boom of a Sharps. The old goat was keeping his end up but it seemed like he had competition.

The glare of the fire was not so bright now, but little leaping flames still ate voraciously at everything they could find; spurting, licking and snapping they kept travelling. Their glare had died down but every now and then as timber parted or embers hissed everything was thrown in sharp relief once more. Then the shadows lengthened again. Pretty soon, however, the flames left behind them the smouldering ruins of the stables and feed-barn and began to go up on the other building and really get to work on it.

The glare became intensified again. The stable-youth rose to his knees and began to crawl aimlessly. The wounded man in the clearing squirmed feebly. Tom heard him groan. He looked down at the fat bulk of the cook at the foot of the steps. He was still as death. So was his pard who had been tossed beside him.

Furniture crashed over inside the house. Maybe the drifting smoke, the sound of crackling wood, was making the gunman panicky. Then another sound made Tom turn swiftly; instinct made him duck. Bullets whistled over his head. He fired back at Matt Hapwood, standing at the end of the verandah. The big ramrod dodged out of sight around the corner.

Flattening himself against the wall, Tom began to work his way along. He moved away from the door. The tip of Hapwood's hat showed around the corner. Tom fired. The hat came into sight, was suspended comically in the air, then swooped to the ground.

Boot heels thudded. A man ran out on to the verandah. Smoke trails followed him. He turned, facing Tom, triggering madly. The big red-beard fired coolly back. The man teetered on his heels then fell backwards down the steps. He hit the spongy bulk of the cook and bounced. He hit the ground again and rose to one knee. Tom moved and fired again. The other's slug smacked into the wall where Tom's head had been. The gunny clawed at his throat then pitched forward on his face.

Suddenly, a searing pain tore into Tom Heineman's side.

He staggered. The wall held him as he fell to his knees, his gun swinging around mechanically, his thumb jerking the hammer. Matt Hapwood dodged out of sight again. He was too yellow to stop there and finish the job. He had gotten in cover again.

Tom cursed him in a harsh choking voice. 'Come out an' show yourself, you yellow-bellied bastard,' he said.

He kept his gun trained on the corner, willing the arm from which the strength was ebbing to keep up there, to keep in line. His eyelids began to droop, everything was smoky. When he held his eyes wide-open they smarted. The corner of the house was like a black line in front of the sight of his gun. If anything moved out of that line he would press the trigger.

He heard hoofbeats. If that was Loop W night riders coming in everything was finished. He heard Hapwood's boot heels thudding around the corner, going away.

Tom staggered through the gap in the verandah rail. He fell, then rose and went forward again, a huge bearded monster wreathed in smoke, the lurid glare behind etching his figure in bold terrible relief.

'Mike!' he yelled. 'Mike.'

His voice got weaker, it was a mere croak when Doc Greaves dismounted beside him and caught him in his arms.

'I'm here, Tom,' he said. 'It's Mike, Tom. Take it easy.'

The doctor grunted as his huge burden became a dead-weight. He sank to his knees lowering Tom with him until the shaggy, leonine head was cradled there. His hands were bathed in blood.

The sheriff and his men were being led away by a gesticulating, yelling old man. Then the old man came back and dropped on his knees beside the doctor and his unconscious burden.

'How is he?' he said.

'Pretty far gone I guess,' said Doc Greaves. 'Will you give me a hand to take him somewhere. If I can get him on a couch or something I may be able to do something for him. He may have a chance.'

The oldster pointed. 'Matt Hapwood's cabin,' he said. 'There's a couch in there. The fire's petering out. It won't reach that far.'

Meanwhile Hapwood himself was running breathlessly across the clearing in front of the big ranch house.

'All right, Matt,' barked a voice from the shadows of the verandah.

Hapwood stopped in his tracks, turned, his hand snaking down to his gun.

The figure on the steps blurred into motion too. Smoke and flame spurted from the lean man's hip. A slug drilled Hapwood's shoulder, spinning him around. He straightened, mouthing curses.

The lean man was limping down the verandah steps;

158

his yellow hair glinted in the reflected glow of the fire. Mad with pain and rage Hapwood fired again with both guns.

The lean man did not flinch. He kept on coming. Both his guns were out now, held at waist level. They crashed and flamed. Hapwood's big body shook. Then it seemed to shrink as life was blasted out of it and it was only a shapeless bundle in the dirt of the yard.

Judy Maxton came running down the steps calling: 'Mack! Mack!'

She ran to him, arms outflung. He holstered his still-smoking guns and caught her.

'It was him or me, Judy,' he said tonelessly.

'I know! I know! You – are you all right?'

He stroked her hair gently. 'Yes, little *chiquita*, I'm all right.'

Sheriff Clem Poynton came running towards them. He gave the body a cursory glance.

'We got 'em all,' he said. 'The boys are gonna run 'em off. The old-timer's all right, but your big pardner's hurt bad. He's in Hapwood's cabin. The doc's with him.'

'Come on, Judy,' said the young man.

She ran fast to keep up with his loping strides.

They entered the cabin. Panhandle Muggins and Doc Greaves were standing beside the couch on which lay the huge, still red-bearded figure. Big Tom was conscious.

'He was waiting for you, Mack,' the doctor said. Mack knew by his voice what he meant.

The big man's hand groped feebly. The young man grasped it as he went on his knees beside the low couch.

Tom was trying to talk. Mack went nearer. The whispered words came one by one: 'Where's the girl?'

Mack motioned to Judy and she came and stood by the

bed. Her eyes were bright with tears as she looked down at the dying man.

His fading eyes sought her face. For a moment they seemed to be fixed as if they saw right into her. The leonine redhead nodded almost imperceptibly and the whispered voice said: 'I wish you both … best … of luck.' Then the eyes closed.

Mack stood up, put his arm around Judy's shoulders and led her away. Doc Greaves came forward and reverently placed a pure white bandanna over the dead face of his old friend.

The young couple, close together, walked slowly across the clearing. With a sweep of his arm Mack indicated the glowing wreckage around them.

'All this will be rebuilt,' he said. Then he became silent. Judy clung to him. The deadly fear of losing each other was like a sword prising them apart.

Sheriff Clem Poynton came towards them once more. Mack let Judy go but she still clung to his hand. They stood still and waited for the sheriff.

The portly man looked a little grimy and his black walrus moustache drooped a little more than usual.

He stopped dead in front of Mack. Then he stuck out his hand. His voice was gruff as he said: 'I guess I gotta congratulate the new ramrod of the Loop W.'

Mack shook the hand. 'Thanks, Sheriff.'

Judy's soft voice echoed his words.

Sheriff Poynton stepped back a little. 'I'm a plain-spoken man, young feller,' he said. 'There's no need atall fer that face fungus of yourn. If you'll take my advice you'll shave it off before the wedding.'